ONE BOSSY ARRANGEMENT

AN ENEMIES TO LOVERS ARRANGED MARRIAGE ROMANCE

RUBY EMHART

ABOUT THE BOOK

Mysterious stranger that took my v-card turned out be my betrothed.
I'm planning to run, but now I'm having his baby.

Sleeping with a man of my choosing is forbidden.
And would piss off Daddy, but that's exactly what I did.
I gave myself to a scorching hot stranger.
And he gifted me a night to remember.

Later I find out that he's Marcello DeLuca.
Bossy, possessive, and *dangerous AF.*
Not only is he keeping me from my dream business.
But he's the one I'm arranged to marry.

His wicked world sends shivers down my spine.
Just as I plot my escape, his velvety, deep voice ropes me in.
A slight brush of his skin makes my body tingle with desire.
And leaves me begging for more.

Even then, if he thinks I'm going to walk down the aisle for him,
he better think again.

Until...
I find out *his baby is growing inside me.*

WARNING

CONTENTS

ALSO BY RUBY EMHART

CHAPTER ONE

MILA

"FOR FUCK'S SAKE, Harper. You have a bedroom for that," I scoffed as I stormed into our small apartment and slammed the door shut. My roommate and best friend, Harper, was straddling her shirtless boyfriend on the couch, cheeks flushed, and hair mussed.

"You weren't supposed to be here for another hour," Harper admitted as she moved off Jacob's lap and plopped onto the cushion, trying to flatten her auburn hair back into place.

I tossed my keys onto the tiny table by the door and dropped my bag on the floor with a thud before heading to the kitchen. I had a foul taste in my mouth and needed a drink. My day had just turned to shit, and the last thing I wanted to see was my friend getting down with her boyfriend in our living room.

Jacob rose from the couch with a look of unease at my obvious crap mood, pulled on his t-shirt, and bent down to kiss Harper.

"See ya later, babe," he said before turning to me on his way out. "Nice seeing you, as always, Mila."

"Call me," Harper called out as he left.

As soon as he closed the door, I turned with a pointed look at my best friend, crossing my arms in front of me.

"What's up your ass?" Harper asked as I walked by the couch and into the kitchen.

"You wouldn't believe me if I told you," I answered.

"Try me. I haven't seen you this bothered in... well, ever," Harper stated.

I grabbed the bottle of Jim Beam from the cabinet above our stove and walked back to the living room, plopping on the couch next to my friend. I felt her eyes on me as I removed the cap and took a swig straight from the bottle, hissing as it burned all the way down.

"So, we're drinking in the middle of the day now?" Harper asked as she grabbed the bottle from me to take her own drink.

"Believe me, my news merits some numbing," I answered dryly.

"Lay it on me."

"I just got a call from my mother. She was sweet enough to remind me that I am getting married in two weeks." I grabbed the bottle back to take another gulp of alcohol.

"You're going through with it?" Harper asked.

"I don't have a choice."

I opened up to Harper during our first year at UCLA and told her everything about my family and who we were. That when I turned eighteen my father decided it was in the best interest of our family for me to marry the son of his business partner to strengthen their power in the business community. So, without my consent, they promised me to Marcello DeLuca.

"There has to be something you can do. Anya got out of it. Why can't you?" Harper asked.

"With me being the only heiress now that she married Camden, I am obligated, and you don't tell Don Aleksander Fedorov no," I answered grumpily.

"Well, is he at least hot?" Harper teased.

"I wouldn't know. The engagement ceremony was done by proxy. But I do know he dated my sister when I was in high school, which makes everything even more ridiculous and unappealing. Who wants their sister's sloppy seconds?" I scowled.

The more I thought about things, the more irritated I became. I followed every rule my parents gave me in hopes they would change their mind. My naïve little heart thought I could get out of it somehow. If I could get away from it all, just disappear and start fresh with a new name, I could live the life I dreamed of. I could be free from my father and the mafia forever.

"If Anya dated him, how do you not know what he looks like?" Harper asked.

"We're four years apart. I was in middle school when they dated, and she never brought him around to the house. I left for Russia before high school and started living with my grandmother. I'm sure he was at some of the big gatherings when I would visit for the holidays, but I always stuck to myself and didn't try to get to know anyone. When I came home for college, I made it a point to stay as far away from there as possible."

"You really want nothing to do with that kind of life, huh?"

I shrugged my shoulders, not feeling like I was missing out by staying away from my family. I did it to protect myself and try to have the life I wanted, not the life my family expected me to have. "I need to disappear," I said aloud.

"Yeah, right," Harper scoffed.

"No, Harper, I'm serious." I turned to face Harper, mirroring her on the couch. "I have two weeks to get out of here and never look back. You could come with me."

"Wouldn't your family just hunt you down and bring you back?"

"Not if they can't find me. I know people. I could get new credentials and disappear altogether. Like witness protection."

Harper narrowed her eyes at me, deciding if I was being serious or just losing my damn mind. She twisted her lips in consideration before clicking her tongue and answering, "I'm in. Let's do it. Where are we going?"

"You're amazing," I gushed as I leaned over and gave her a huge hug.

My phone started ringing from my purse on the floor, but I ignored it, knowing who it was. Avoidance was the first part of my escape plan.

"So, where are we headed?" Harper asked, not questioning why I wasn't picking up the ringing phone.

"I think New York would be good. It's a huge city, and it will be easy to get lost. We just need to get it all planned out and leave right before the wedding. We can't let anyone find out."

"I've always wanted to visit New York," Harper voiced. My phone rang again, and this time, she gave me a pointed look. "Answer it."

"It's just Anya waiting for us downtown for some celebratory drinks. We were supposed to be there twenty minutes ago." I offered a fake smile as my friend shook her head at me.

"You can't just ignore her. She will end up at our door with your dad's goons. Just answer it and tell her we're on our way. We'll pacify her for now and plan later."

I rolled my eyes and groaned but did as she suggested. She wasn't wrong about Anya showing up with an entourage, and that was the last thing I needed. I told my sister we were on our way, and within twenty minutes, we were at a swanky, high-end bar in downtown Los Angeles I had never been to. Once Harper and I were inside, we saw and heard Anya waving and calling for us from a couch right in the center of the bar.

"Here we go," I muttered under my breath as we made our way over.

"Mila!" Anya shrieked as she pulled me into a tight hug. "Harper."

We all sat and grabbed a drink from the table that Anya had already ordered. I was somewhat listening to them discuss wedding plans and shopping for my dress, but I was trying to drown them out as I looked around the bar. I hated to hear my sister talking about it as though I was marrying prince charming and not her ex whom I was being forced to be with.

"Earth to Mila," Anya sang from across the table.

"Sorry," I lied. "What were you saying?"

"I was telling Harper that we have an appointment at a dress shop down the street at five," Anya answered.

"Yippie," I said dryly before taking another drink.

"Mila, you need to cooperate with me here. Daddy-" her sentence was interrupted by her phone vibrating on the table. "Hold on."

When she answered, her shoulders sagged. I could tell it was Camden, and I could only guess he needed her help with my nephew. She hung up the phone and gave us an exaggerated pout.

"I gotta go, girls. Micha is proving to be a tad too much for Camden to handle alone." She rolled her eyes and downed the rest of her martini as she rose from the couch. "The drinks are paid for, but make sure you get to that appointment at five. I'll call later to let you know all you will need."

"Please don't," I answered.

"Just do it, Mila. You'll regret fighting Daddy on this," she said before kissing me on the cheek.

She waved bye to Harper and hurried out of the bar without another word. I finished my drink and grabbed another that was already on the table, finishing off half of it.

"We aren't going to that appointment, are we?" Harper asked.

"I'd rather chew my arm off."

"Mila's gonna have your ass for missing that appointment."

"Eh, she'll live."

We laughed as we finished our drinks and talked about everything and nothing. The night got away from us as we indulged in drinks and chatting with random people that came and went. I ran to the bathroom, and as I made my way back to Harper, I looked through angry texts from Anya about missing my dress fitting appointment. I was too distracted to notice I was at the wrong table and started to sit down, landing in someone's lap. Assuming it was Harper, I leaned back to say something obscene but was met with a handsome man looking at me with amusement.

"Comfortable?" he asked with a smirk.

It took way too long for me to register that I was sitting in a strange man's lap, but when I did, I sucked in a sharp breath and rose to my feet, a touch too quick. I stumbled and started to fall, but strong arms caught me mid-air.

"Easy there, bella," he chuckled.

I steadied myself and moved out of his arms. I

could feel my cheeks flush with embarrassment. He was tall, dark, and handsome with a touch of danger under the surface. His voice was velvety and deep, and I couldn't take my eyes off him. The scent of his cologne mixed in with cedar was encasing me, pulling me in more and more.

"Sorry, I thought this was where my friend was sitting," I offered, looking around for Harper.

"You can sit in my lap any time you want."

My mouth hung open at his response. Normally, I would be annoyed with such a statement, but there was something about the way he said it that made me want to jump in his arms. My body tingled all over as I watched his eyes rake over my body then back up to mine with a hooded look that screamed sex and danger. For some reason, I loved it.

"Can I buy you a drink?"

"Yes." I shocked myself at my quick answer.

He motioned for me to sit, and I obliged. He sat next to me, not leaving much room between us. I searched around the bar for Harper and finally saw her a few feet away with Jacob's face buried in her neck. They had no shame.

"What are you drinking, bella?"

"It's Mila, and I'll have a water and a long island."

"I'm Marc," he responded with a smile before hailing a server to order our drinks.

I was hyper aware of our legs touching. Excitement ran through my body as I tried my best to calm my racing heart.

"So, what do you do, Mila?"

"Small talk? Really?"

My confidence was growing the more I could feel the invisible pull between us, and the more drinks I consumed. I knew I was marrying someone in two weeks, but I was also desperate to gain some form of control over my life. Sleeping with a man of my choosing was forbidden and would piss off the don, meaning that was exactly what I was going to do.

"You're not a fan of small talk?"

"Not really. I was hoping you'd show me your place instead." My heart pounded in my ears, but I tried to act confident and seductive.

"My suite is on the top floor," he answered. I looked at him quizzically, making him laugh. "I own the building."

"Lead the way," I answered without hesitation, surprising myself.

He grabbed my hand and led me to an elevator hidden in the back of the bar. On the ride up, I sent a quick text to Harper, letting her know I would see her at home and that I would explain later. When the doors opened on the top floor, I was in awe. It was an open floorplan with windows filling the wall facing Rodeo Drive. It was sleek and obviously owned by a man, but somehow cozy at the same time.

Without a word, Marc pinned me against the wall and kissed me hard and fast, instantly sending a fire to my belly. I didn't fight it. I had never been kissed that way, and I loved the way it made me feel wanted. When we broke free, we were both panting. We just stood there with my back against the wall and his hands on each side of my head.

"Take off your clothes, bella," he said in a raw, husky voice. I looked at him like a deer in headlights. I had asked to be here, but my own inexperience suddenly made me panic. I bit my lip, not wanting to tell the truth only Harper knew. He pulled my lip free with his thumb. "What is it, bella?"

After a moment, I decided to be honest. "I...I've never done this."

"What? Slept with a stranger?"

"With anyone," I whispered.

"You're a virgin?"

I nodded my head, expecting him to be upset, to make fun of me for being a virgin at twenty-two. Instead, he growled and kissed me again with the kind of passion I dreamed about, the kind I read about in books and saw in movies. My body responded to him without me having to think about what I was doing as I pulled him to me. I could feel his hard cock rubbing against me, and it made me so damn wet.

He pulled off my top, instantly grasping my breasts in each hand, kissing the flesh above my bra. I tugged at his shirt, needing him to be as exposed as I felt. He broke our connection and stepped back as he pulled his shirt off. He then quickly stepped out of his shoes as he unbuckled his belt.

"Take off your shorts," he demanded.

I did as I was told and dropped the fabric around my ankles before stepping out of them, excitement pulsing through me. I kicked my shoes to the side and took in the sight in front of me. Marc stood in the moonlight of his suite in just his boxer briefs, which left nothing to the imagination. His erection was very evident as it pushed against the cotton. He smiled at my gawking mouth before stripping out of his boxers, letting his massive cock swing free.

"Jesus," I breathed. I all but drooled as I took in his size while vaguely wondering how he would even fit.

"Are you sure you want to do this, bella?" I nodded my head eagerly. "Then take off the rest of your clothes. I want to see you."

I removed my bra and panties and stood with confidence in my nudity, thanking the stars above for the liquid courage. I knew how I looked but had never been so exposed.

"You're so fucking beautiful," he said matter of fact.

He grabbed my hand and led me to his bedroom, sitting me on the edge of his bed. He dropped to his knees before me and spread my legs apart to lick me between my folds. My head fell back, and I moaned loudly. He scooted my ass closer to the edge of the bed, spreading my lips apart as he dove his tongue inside me, making me cry out. I had never felt such an intense sensation. My hips automatically gyrated with his motions, begging for him to keep going.

He sucked on my overly sensitive clit as he slid a finger inside of me, then another.

"Holy shit," I cried out as he pumped his fingers in and out of me, licking and sucking.

He growled in response but didn't move his head to speak. His pace quickened, and I felt my body tense in a delicious way. Before I knew it, I was screaming out as my pussy clenched around his fingers with an intense orgasm, and I started seeing stars. I let myself fall back on his bed to catch my breath as he removed his fingers and kissed the inside of my thigh. When I looked down at him, he stuck his fingers in his mouth and sucked them clean.

Who the hell is this man?

"Are you okay?" he asked with a smirk. He knew good and well how I was doing.

I smiled in response, not yet able to speak. I just had my first orgasm, and he hadn't disappointed. Harper had told me repeatedly that I was missing out, but I thought she was bullshitting. Clearly, I was wrong.

"Don't get too relaxed. We aren't done yet," he promised.

My stomach dipped in anticipation. I sat up and smiled at him, biting my bottom lip. He cocked his head as he watched my mouth and climbed over me for another kiss. I could taste myself on his tongue, and it wasn't terrible. It was kind of hot, if I was honest.

He moved us further up the bed, and I wrapped my arms and legs around him, letting myself get lost in the kiss. He trailed kisses down my neck and gave each of my peaks the attention I craved, nipping at each taught nipple. I moaned as the sensation shot a bolt of electricity straight to my eager pussy. He came back up to take my lips to his as he slid two fingers back inside me.

"You're still so fucking wet, Mila," he groaned. "I hope you're ready, because I've wanted to bury myself inside you the moment you sat in my lap."

Holy, mother of God. Is this really happening? My heart was pounding in my chest, and I was sure he could hear it. He looked into my eyes as he lined himself up at my opening and gently pushed himself in. I sucked in a sharp breath at the sheer size of him filling me up. He rested for a moment so that I could adjust to him, watching me for the go-ahead.

I nodded my head to let him know I was okay to keep going, and he slid back slightly, then back in as far as he could go. I felt a sharp pinch but didn't want to stop.

He feathered kisses over my face as he slowly pumped in and out of me, the pain fading into pleasure. "Relax, bella. I've got you," he whispered as he started to speed up his movements.

In no time, I was moving in sync with him. He kissed me with so much passion that my head started to spin. He pumped his rock-hard cock faster inside of me, and I felt the same sensations as before when I was ready to come. His room was filled with our moans and labored breathing as we moved in unison, bringing each other closer to our climax. I felt myself clench around him, and he moaned, pounding even faster inside me until we were both yelling out with our orgasms.

He kissed me lightly as we both came down and tried to catch our breath. Then he carefully pulled out of me to lay beside me, pulling me into him as we both drifted off to sleep, thoroughly exhausted.

When I woke, it was just after midnight, and Marc was still asleep. I crept out of the bed, careful not to wake him, in search of my clothes. I needed to get home before Harper started freaking out. As I got dressed, I happened to see a black credit card lying on the coffee table and panicked when I saw the name.

Marcello DeLuca.

"No fucking way."

CHAPTER
TWO
MILA

ONE OF MY biggest dreams is to own my own music company. Ever since I was little. My grandmother always made sure I had an outlet when things got stressful or I needed to be scarce while my father handled business. I was always grateful when she would visit from Russia with new sheet music to learn. I was drawn to music right away. I learned all I could about the history of music in addition to as many instruments as possible and how to play many of them.

I had met a man through my father's long line of business acquaintances, George Martin, who had ties in the music industry and wanted to help me get my own record company up and running as well as backing the start-ups costs. I was grateful for his interest, especially when my father refused to help me because he thought starting my own business in something so unreliable to be pointless. Since my sister had married outside of the mafia syndicate, our father looked to me as next in line to run things, and he already had his business ventures concrete and profitable. He didn't see a need to add more to it, even though it was my dream. But I refused to listen to him and worked with George in secret.

George and I worked together on and off during my last two years in college. He had a little over ten years' experience in the industry and offered a lot of knowledge, saving me from having to learn by crashing and burning. At first, he helped purchase some equipment to record my own music while we waited to secure space for a studio. He ensured me he had everything handled so that I could focus on school and creating music. But no matter how far he got in the process, he always seemed to hit a wall before we could even start. He never went into detail about the hurdles we had to jump over or why it was so difficult to establish a storefront or license other than saying Marcello DeLuca and my father's board kept refusing every offer and business plan he presented. When I asked George why Marcello would step in to stop progress, he had told me there was a big misunderstanding a few years back with the DeLuca clan, but they had been making his life hell ever since. I was too focused on finishing school to look into it further, and I still refused to go to my father, even though he would have the answers. I was determined to make my own way without his help.

Learning about Marcello threw a new wrench in everything, but I was determined to find a way around him as well.

It wasn't until my mother reminded me of who I was to marry that I saw the connection. I was supposed to marry the man keeping me from my dreams in two weeks. Not only that, but I also ended up handing over my virginity to him, not knowing who he was. So, in a way, he stole that too. I had made that choice to take control of my life. A part of me wondered if he knew who I was the whole damn time, making me even more upset about the entire situation.

"Planning on eating that or building with it?" Harper's voice broke me out of my thoughts. I was instantly surrounded by the smell of my eggs burning.

"Shit," I hissed, tossing the pan off the burner and turning the dial off.

"Let's just go with cereal this morning," my friend suggested as she pulled a box from the top of the fridge. She retrieved two bowls and spoons as I grabbed the milk, and we sat at the small kitchen table. "Want to talk about it?"

"I fucked up, Harper."

"How so?"

"Remember the guy from last night?"

"You mean the strange man you spent the night with and who you handed over your forbidden fruit to?" Harper teased.

"First off, he wasn't strange. He was ungodly handsome and charming to boot," I defended.

"And secondly?"

"Despite his sex appeal and the way he made me feel so safe, he is in fact the devil incarnate."

Harper snorted around a mouthful of cereal. "What are you talking about?"

"It was Marcello." Harper looked at me in confusion. "My husband-to-be," I added to help her connect the dots. "He also happens to be the reason George and I can't get the business up and running."

"No shit? Did he know who you were?"

"I mean, he had to, right? It's too much of a coincidence."

Harper scrunched her brows in thought as we ate in

silence. I was so torn. I kept getting flashbacks of his chiseled, muscular body moving over me as he feathered kisses all over my face, but then the harsh reminder of who he was made those memories feel dirty and wrong.

My phone started to ring, breaking the silence. I knew it would either be Anya to yell at me some more or my mother. My head was pounding from the alcohol I had sucked down the night before, and I didn't need to add to it by listening to their bullshit. I hated that they were so on board with me marrying Marcello and didn't once ask me what I wanted. The ringing was incessant, and both Harper and I were over it. I could have just turned my phone off, but I knew that would give them motive to come to the apartment, which would be worse than dealing with them over the phone.

I finally looked at my phone to see who it was, and I was right. It was my sister.

"What, Anya?" I wasn't in the mood to be cordial.

"We are having dinner tonight at the house with your future in-laws. Be there at seven."

"Anya, I-" she hung up before I could finish. I had no desire to have dinner with my family, much less with the DeLuca's.

"I take it she's still pissed?" Harper asked, rising to put her bowl in the sink.

"Yep. She called to tell me there is a dinner tonight at my parents with the future in-laws. She obviously didn't give me an opportunity to argue or refuse."

"You could just not go," Harper suggested.

"We both know that's not an option. Especially after I flaked on the dress fitting, which I'm sure has already been rescheduled. I wouldn't be surprised if both my sister and mother escorted me there to make sure I played my part as the blushing bride."

"The story of your life is something else."

"Trust me, I know."

"Want backup to this dinner?"

"Thanks for the offer, but no. They won't want outsiders there. No offense."

"All the offense taken," Harper gasped in mock shock. "They are going to have to accept me eventually. I'm not going anywhere, mafia princess or not."

I waited as long as I could before getting ready for dinner. I was not looking forward to it, but I was also anxious to see Marc again. No, not Marc. Marcello. I hated that I *wanted* to see him again, despite knowing who he was. I just wanted to go back to the night before and bask in my ignorant bliss.

I decided to wear a simple black dress as a symbolism of my life coming to an end. Metaphorically, of course. I hoped my family would catch on but decided it was fine, even if they didn't. I kept my hair down in loose curls and wore minimal makeup. I wanted to look decent while not showing that I had made too much of an effort. I knew it would piss my mother off, making me smile.

My phone pinged, altering me to the car waiting downstairs. I rolled the window down as we drove through LA, loving the cool April evening air washing over my face. I needed to find balance before walking into my parents' place and to mentally prepare myself for anything. I knew I needed to play nice while Harper and I made plans to get me out of LA before the wedding so that no one suspected I was planning to run. I would go along with the preparations, but I wouldn't hide my hatred for the future they had planned for me. They would expect it.

My heart started racing as we entered the large gates of my family's home and rounded the large fountain, stopping at the front door. Marcello was on the other side of the door, and my body betrayed me as I felt excited to see him.

I was greeted by our housekeeper, Mariana, just as I walked in.

"Hola, Mila. So good to see you," Mariana gushed, giving me a hug. My parents hated that I was so close to her. When I was little, she would also help with the nanny role to Anya and I. Although I looked at her like family, everyone else couldn't see past her role in keeping the house functional.

"Hola, Mariana. How are the kids?"

Before she could answer, my mother rounded the corner with Anya on her tail. Mariana nodded to me and scurried away before my mother could scold her.

"Stop chatting with the help, Mila. You have guests waiting."

"Good evening, Mama," I offered as she kissed me on each cheek. The tradition was meant to be a warm welcome, but I could feel the iciness of her lips.

"Come to the dining room. Everyone is already seated," she said as she walked away.

My mother was beautiful, and she knew it. Her hair was silky black and reached the middle of her back. She was tall and slender and always dressed to impress, even if she never left the house. She was an icon within the mafia families, but she was also known for being cold and calculated. Some would say she needed to be that way as the wife to the Don, but I didn't buy it.

"Don't mind her," Anya whispered to me as she wound her arm into mine and led me to the grandiose dining room. "She's just stressed over the wedding."

"*She's* stressed?" I hissed to my sister, who just clicked her tongue and gave me the side-eye as we entered the room.

There was a large dark walnut table in the center that could seat twenty people. Food was perfectly placed in the center with large candelabras mixed in. My father was seated at the head of the table, my mother at the opposite end. On one side of the table sat four men I could only assume were the DeLuca family, although Marcello was missing. On the other side sat Anya, Camden, and my nephew. Two seats at the end by my father were empty, which I assumed were for Marcello and myself. I quietly made my way to the seat by my father, trying to ignore the eyes on me. I leaned down to kiss his cheek before sitting down.

"Good evening, Papa."

"We've been waiting," he boomed, startling me.

"I was told dinner was at seven. It's a quarter to," I answered.

My father just stared at me, letting me know I was out of line to talk back. I used to admire him until I learned who he really was and he forced me to lead a life I wanted nothing to do with. His jet-black hair was lined with white at the sides, giving away his age. His face was peppered with stubble, and his jawline sharp. He looked the part as the Don and could strike fear into anyone with one look. Unfortunately for him, I knew all of his looks, and they didn't scare me.

It was then that Marcello strolled into the dining room in a sharp midnight blue suit. My heart started racing, and my palms began to sweat the moment we locked eyes. I could have sworn I saw a hint of surprise when he saw me, but I could have been mistaken as he wore a mask of a mixture of confidence and indifference. He mussed the hair of the younger man at the table, who looked to be around my age, earning him a nasty look, but he just chuckled as he took the seat across from me.

"Now that we are all here, I will introduce everyone," my father started. Everyone gave him his full attention. "Mila, this is your future husband, Marcello DeLuca."

I locked eyes on Marcello and felt my cheeks redden instantly. He raised an eyebrow and smirked as my father continued.

"Next to him is his youngest brother, Dominic. Then Dante and Cristiano." Each man nodded at me without saying a word. I was taken back that one of them looked almost identical to Marcello. He was slightly shorter with longer hair, but other than that, they were identical. "At the end, next to your mother, is their father, Antonio DeLuca."

"Welcome to the family, Mila," Antonio offered as he raised his glass of wine.

Everyone followed suit and waited for me to raise my glass. I hesitated for a moment, glancing back to see Marc watching me closely. I ground my teeth when the feeling of hatred and betrayal washed over me. Something about the way he looked at me made me feel as though he knew exactly who I was when we met at the bar and that he was victorious in getting me into bed so easily. Finally, I raised my glass and smiled as sweet as honey to everyone at the table.

"Thank you," I said loud enough for everyone to hear, and we all took a drink from our glasses.

"Let's eat!" my father exclaimed, and everyone started to fill their plates.

I watched as small talk started between everyone as I remained silent. It was clear there was already some kind of repour or friendship between the DeLuca's and the Fedorov's, which made the evening worse. I was the only one who had no idea who these men were, other than seeing them at large gatherings here and there. When I looked back at Marcello, he was looking at my sister with an expression of admiration, making me frown a little. *Did he still have feelings for her? Did he think that by marrying me he would get closer to her?* My line of thinking only pissed me off more. *Was I some pawn in this fucking game?*

"Eat, Mila," my father snapped from beside me.

I obliged by placing a small piece of chicken on my plate with some fettuccine. My stomach was in knots, and I knew I wouldn't be able to eat much. I didn't want to show my emotions, so I kept my eyes on my plate as I picked small bites here and there. My family was talking to the DeLuca's as though these dinners were normal. Perhaps they were. I had made a point to stay out of the family business, but now I felt like a fish out of water and kept replaying my night in Marc's suite over and over in my head.

"Do you not like the food, bella?" Marc's voice carried over the table and chatter, landing right in my panties and making them wet instantly. *How the hell can his voice alone have that effect on me?*

"I like the food just fine," I answered with a hint of anger. "It's the company that isn't sitting well with me."

"Watch your tone," my father snapped.

I kept my mouth shut as I glared at Marc, who didn't take his eyes off of me as he popped a piece of chicken into his mouth.

"You will respect your husband, especially in the presence of others," my father spat.

At that, my blood boiled. "He's not my husband yet, is he?" I looked to my father in defiance. "I will go along with your asinine union, but I refuse to show respect when I have received none in return."

My father slammed his hand down on the table, making me jump, and the entire table grew silent. "You will watch how you speak to me in my own home," he boomed. "Remember your place, Mila."

I opened my mouth to respond but was kicked under the table by Marcello.

"That's enough, Mila," my mother chimed in from the other end of the table. "We have guests, and you will conduct yourself accordingly."

I stared at her for a moment, then looked back down at my plate. Everyone started talking again, but I felt all eyes on me. I looked up to see Marc glaring at me. I scowled back at him and ate my meal in silence.

The rest of dinner was a bit of a blur. Between my emotions playing tug of war on my insides, I was forced to play the part of the perfect daughter to keep the peace and show I can fall in line. And I hated every second of it. Though, my anger subsided slightly watching Marc laughing and teasing his brothers. Camden even got into the action as Anya laughed and chided in when appropriate. My mother and Antonio spoke quietly, not paying attention to any of it, making me wonder what they could be discussing. I had no idea she was as close as she seemed to be with Marcello's father.

I watched on, wondering if I could really enjoy this life. However, I knew that I was only seeing the brighter side of things. I knew it could get dark very quickly, and I wasn't sure I was cut out for it. I found myself imagining a life with the man I met at the bar and whether that was a façade or the real Marcello. In the same thought process, I reminded myself that he was the son of a mafia leader and the man keeping me from my dreams. From the life I wanted.

How could I ever fall in love with a man I was forced to be with and who expected me to be someone I'm not, nor ever wanted to be?

CHAPTER
THREE
MARCELLO

MY LIFE WAS FUCKING chaotic without a moment to find peace or joy. My father trusted me with enforcing most of our business deals, and it wasn't always rainbows and kittens. My name was known and feared for a good reason. My oldest brother, Cristiano, was our father's right-hand man. With our father getting ready to step down, he made Cristiano the decision maker and the face of our business. He was also the most level-headed of us DeLuca boys.

Dante was older than me by ten minutes. We were the next in line, but he was more of a jokester and channeled his anger better than the rest of us. He always wanted to have a good time but would kick someone's ass just for disrespecting any of us, and he would do it with ease. He was with me a good deal of the time and the one I would trust with my life. Our baby brother was Dominic and was still learning the ropes. At first, he hated being tied to the mafia and all it entailed. He wasn't too worried about any of it, knowing he had three older brothers ahead of him before he had any real responsibility. However, our father wouldn't let him walk away from this life. He made sure to tie him in, even if it was little things here and there. I hated to see him so unhappy, but it was part of being a DeLuca. Happiness was the farthest thing from our minds and goals.

I always thought with certainty that I would marry Anya. She was my first love in high school, and as the eldest daughter, it made sense she would be my wife. But as we got older, it was clear we were headed in different directions. When I heard she was marrying Camden, I was both sad and happy for her. I wanted the best for her, and if that meant marrying another man, then so be it. It was a surprise when my father told me I would marry Anya's sister, no matter what I thought about it. We needed to tie our family to the Fedorov's, and she was the only way.

I was twenty-four at the time of our engagement and went on with my life, not thinking too much about it. I had to focus on my responsibilities, which didn't leave much room to think about marriage. It was just another duty to the family. So I buried myself in work and numbed myself with alcohol and women. There were many things I did and saw that I wanted to forget. I was seeking some comfort the night I met Mila, and something changed in me. I never bothered to remember the name of Anya's sister and had no idea she was the beauty who caught my attention at the bar. The way she had looked at me and got right to the point in what she wanted set me on fire. She was different than other women, and I needed to have her.

When I saw her sitting next to Don Aleksander Fedorov, my heart jumped into my fucking throat. I tried to play it off but was finding it tough. As I watched her through dinner, I was reminded of her perfect naked body writhing under me. I could still smell her arousal and feel the walls of her sweet, tight pussy clench around my cock. Just the thought made me excited, and I was grateful for the table hiding it.

Everyone was done with dinner and just chatting while enjoying dessert. Dominic had left the table to take a personal call, and Dante took his seat, right next to me.

"So, Marc...who's the flavor of the week?"

I looked at Mila before turning to my brother, happy to see his question caught her attention.

"You know, I sampled a sweet, tight piece just last night that I can't wait to sample again."

Dante's grin widened as he raised his eyebrows. His dark brown hair matched our late mother's, as well as his bright green eyes. The rest of his features matched our father's. He was just an inch shorter than me with serious athletic build. He would have been a great baseball star if our father had let him follow his dream.

The sound of silverware clinging against a plate filled the room, catching everyone's attention. We all looked over to see Mila scooting her chair back and rising from the table.

"Excuse me," she said before rushing out of the room.

I watched her walk away, loving the way her black dress hugged her ass. I licked my lips at the thought of seeing it in my hands.

"What's got her all twisted?" Dante asked with a smirk, knowing damn well what she was upset about.

"Good job," I whispered with sarcasm before leaving my own seat to chase Mila down.

I heard her heels down the hall in the direction of the restroom and followed the sound. The door was just closing as I rounded the corner. I pushed it open before she had the chance to close it and lock me out. I needed to feel her, to taste her. When I was in the restroom, I shut the door and locked it. She spun around, at first in shock, then anger crossed her face.

"What the fuck are you doing?"

"Your ass looks so fucking delectable in that dress, I opted for a different dessert option." I started walking toward her, but she held her hand up to stop me.

"You're out of your mind. Our families are right in the other room."

"And? It will be fun to see if you can be quiet when you want to scream my name," I answered in a deeper voice.

Seeing her in front of me made me want her even more. Her tits were perky, and her cleavage was peeking out of the top of her dress. It hugged her hips perfectly, reminding me what it was like to have them in my hands. I stepped closer, but she backed herself against the counter.

"Come on, bella. We both know your tight little pussy is soaked right now. I can smell it."

Her face reddened, letting me know I was right. Her hands squeezed the edge of the counter, and I watched as she licked her bottom lip before tucking it under her teeth. For some reason, it made me horny as fuck when she did it. Closing the distance between us, I rested my hands on the counter on either side of her. Our faces were inches apart.

"I've been wanting to taste you from the moment I saw you seated across from me. Just watching you eat made me hard as fuck. Tell me you want me too, Mila," I said huskily with need.

I moved so that our faces were almost touching. She let out a moan, and I instantly took her lips to mine, feeling her melt against me. I ground my already stiffened cock against her sex, and she reached both of her hands down to my ass, pressing me closer to her. I stepped back slightly just to lift her up and set her on the counter. She wound her legs around me and thrusted her hands into my hair.

I broke our kiss to move to her neck, pulling her head back slightly. "Tell me you want me," I growled between kisses.

"I want you," she breathed.

I brought my lips back to hers in an eager and hungry kiss, then reached between her legs and smiled when I felt her soaked panties. "I was right."

"Stop talking," she bit out, pulling me back in for a kiss.

I shoved her panties aside and buried two fingers deep inside her, making her moan loudly. She was wet and ready, making me even harder. I wanted to take her right then and there, but I needed to taste her first.

I knelt in front of her and spread her legs to give me better access. I sucked her sensitive nub as I worked my fingers in and out of her at a fast pace. She leaned back against the mirror, bringing her heels to the edge of the counter, opening her legs wider. I looked up at her as I removed my fingers and dipped my tongue into her hot pussy, sucking up all I could. It was turning me on more to see her face red with passion. She was trying so hard not to yell out that I knew she was close. I quickly inserted my fingers again, hooking them just right to hit her sweet spot as I licked and sucked on her clit, making her cum so hard her entire body spasmed.

I locked eyes with hers as I rose to stand in front of her, sucking on the fingers I had inside of her. She bit her bottom lip again, and I crushed my mouth to hers with a deep kiss, making sure she could taste herself on my tongue. When we separated, I remained between her legs, not letting her get away. I wasn't done with her yet, but I had a burning question that had been bothering me all through dinner.

"What were you playing at the other night, Mila?" I asked in a low voice. "Did you know who I was when you asked me to take you to my suite?"

Her face contorted from euphoria to rage in an instant. She pushed me back and jumped off the counter, adjusting her panties and dress.

"If I'd known you were the sadistic fucking monster whom I am being forced to marry, I never would have given you the time of day. I regret letting you take my virginity, and I wish it never happened," she spat out before storming out of the bathroom, leaving me stunned.

What the fuck just happened?

I met my father and brothers back at one of our main warehouses. We needed to make sure everything was set for the week's shipments and to go over some new developments our father had wanted to look into.

"Keep an eye on Mila Fedorov," I said to one of my men, Shane. He had been on my team for the past two years and had proven himself to be loyal. "Make sure she doesn't do anything stupid, like leave L.A. She's making me a little nervous with our wedding around the corner."

"You got it, boss."

He took off immediately, and Dante came up and clapped me on the shoulder. "I never did say congratulations."

"For what?" I asked.

"Your wedding. That Mila is going to give you a run for your money," he joked.

"Nothing I can't handle," I answered sharply.

I was still bothered and confused by what Mila had said before storming out of the bathroom. She saw me as a terrible person, and I didn't know why. Granted, I had a reputation, but as far as I knew, she was out of the game. She made it a point to not know what was going on with either family. How could she have such ire for me?

"Just another job, aye?"

"Fuck off, Dante. We both know the marriage needs to happen."

"Yeah, but you can't deny she's hot as hell. You could have been paired with worse."

"She despises everything about the mafia. She wants nothing to do with the life, or me. Can't say I blame her."

"Don't let the Don hear you say that," he teased.

"Watch yourself, brother. He might pick your wife for you, too, if you aren't careful."

He clicked his tongue to his teeth. "He couldn't care less who I am with as long as I do as I'm told. I fall under the radar, working so closely with you. He's never had any interest in me. Not like you and Cristiano. He likes me working behind the scenes and being the muscle. You and Cris were bred to lead."

"Be careful saying that out loud. He may hear you," I joked.

Dante shook his head and said goodbye. Then I went to look for my father and found him finishing up with Cristiano in the office. When they heard me approaching, I was called into the room by my father.

"Get in here, Marcello."

I sat in the chair on the other side of the desk my

father was sitting at. He poured two glasses of bourbon and pushed one across to me. I sipped it as he lit a cigar and sat back in his chair, embodying the look of a mafia lord, shrouded with smoke.

"You'll need to tame that Fedorov daughter. She has no respect for her father or what we do. That will carry into your marriage."

"She's not a wild animal. She's a person who's being forced to do something she never agreed to."

"She's the daughter of a fucking legend. He's carved a clear path for her, and the rest of us, since he was a teenager. People in our business quake when he walks into a room. Not only is he a genius when it comes to business, but he's also ruthless when it comes to people defying or disrespecting him or his family. She's known her place and her fate since the moment she could walk and talk and would be naive to go against him."

"Still, she needs to be shown respect before she gives it. I can understand that," I answered back. I watched my father size me up as he took a long draw off his cigar, puffing the smoke out in rings.

"She's got fire, like your mother did."

I was taken back by the way he spoke about my mother. He didn't talk about her often, and I knew it was because he missed her so much. He might be harsh and cruel on the outside, but when it came to my mother, his humanity showed.

"I know you two didn't have a choice in this wedding, but it's a true marriage all the same, and marriage is sacred. You need to treat it as such, which means no more flavors of the week." The way he quoted my brother made me chuckle. I had no idea he had heard us.

"I know. I will do my best to honor you and to

honor her. But I won't treat her like a pawn or as though she doesn't matter."

"She plays a large role in this since she will be taking over for her father and running half the businesses that make this town thrive in tandem with you. We need to strengthen our alliance or we could face losing business. Her father has managed to tip the hat in his favor in terms of business in this area, and if this marriage falls through the cracks because of an uncontrollable daughter, we could lose both a fortune and our legacy. You will need to teach her what her role is, and fast. I refuse to have her mess up decades of work her father and I have accomplished. That kind of spirit can make life interesting, or it can make life hell. It's now on you to guide her down the right path."

"You mean the path that works for you and the Don."

"You know what I mean, Marcello. You're a good man, and I know you'll do right by her and us. I just need you to know what you're up against and what is expected of you. I loved your mother dearly. At times, she would get us into some trouble. She would fight against some of my decisions, and it wasn't always behind closed doors. But the only way we worked was with mutual respect and communication."

"The difference is that you chose each other because you loved one another. We are being forced together with the hope that we don't clash heads and maybe, eventually, love each other."

"Your mother and I started the same way, son. You aren't the first to have an arranged marriage."

I looked at my father, stunned. I had always believed they were a perfect match for each other and had married because they were in love. No one had ever told me it was an arranged marriage.

"You have a lot of your mother in you. I see it more and more every day. I don't doubt you will be a great husband and have the capacity to love Mila. You'll find a balance."

"Thanks, pops."

I left for home with a lot on my mind. I couldn't remember the last time I had an honest conversation with my father. I was also still bothered by Mila's reaction to my asking if she knew me back at the bar. I needed to see her and find out what the hell had made her so angry. She had crawled under my skin already, which was a first. But I couldn't just let it go. I had to know more. I had to know *her* better, and I was determined to do so before saying "I do."

CHAPTER
FOUR

MILA

"OOH, THAT ONE LOOKS AMAZING," Anya gushed.

"You've said that to the last three dresses, Anya," Harper chuckled.

"They all look so good. Mila has the perfect figure for every one of them." My sister turned her attention back to me through the wall of mirrors in front of me. "How will you choose?"

"Anya, I don't care which one I wear. Pick one, so we can get out of here," I answered annoyed. We had been in the dress shop for over an hour, and I was tired of trying on dresses.

"You have to pick out your own wedding dress, silly. It's the most important day of your life."

"No, it's not. It would be if I were marrying the love of my life and on my own terms, but instead, I am marrying a man who I just met and on father's terms," I snapped.

"How about we go with the one you have on?" Harper cut in, trying to keep the drama at a minimum.

Before we left, she had tried to remind me that I

was only going along with things long enough to plan my escape. I agreed to play nicely, but it was not easy. And my confusion about Marcello was making things worse.

Yet again, I gave myself over to Marc, even after I knew who he was. Why did I let that happen? I mean, sure, it felt amazing. The man was a magician with his tongue, but it made me nauseous to think I let him have access to me at my parents' house. He was my enemy. He was the sole reason I was forced out of a life I wanted, but I was mush any time he was around. His voice alone did strange things to me. I needed to stand my ground and not give in to him anymore before I left for New York because I could feel myself falling for him already, and I needed a clear head to pull this off. Not to mention how cliché it felt that I was falling for the man who had taken my virginity.

"What do you think, Mila?" Harper's voice brought me back to earth.

"This one's fine," I shrugged. "It's not too flashy, and it hugs my curves perfectly."

Anya clapped her hands rapidly with a ridiculous smile plastered across her face. She told the salesclerk we would take the dress I had on, and I had to insist we didn't need to make any alterations.

"Listen, I have to change and hurry out for a meeting. I'll talk to you guys later," I said as I stepped off the pedestal.

Anya gave me a quick kiss on the cheek, and she left with Harper. I was happy to have some peace and quiet before my meeting with George Martin. He had messaged me with an address and told me he had landed a space to turn into a studio. He wanted to meet and go over a new game plan to get us licensed. Now that I knew it was Marcello who was blocking our efforts, I thought I would have a better chance of getting things up and running.

I made my way to the dressing room and began to change. I had my back to the curtain of the small space, standing in only my black lace thong panties when I heard the curtain open. When I looked up, I saw Marcello standing behind me, and my heart stopped. *How the fuck did he know I was here?*

"Whoa, I've been thinking about that ass since dinner last night, bella. It looks divine," he said as he grabbed each cheek and stepped closer to kiss my bare shoulder.

I stood still in shock. I couldn't wrap my head around him being here, right after I told myself I wouldn't let him in again. Still, I could feel my body respond to his. *Traitor.*

"What are you doing here, Marc?" I finally bit out as I elbowed him in the gut and turned when he stepped back from the blow. It pissed me off when he laughed.

"I know things, Mila. And since you left me hanging in need, I wanted to see if we could rectify the situation."

He took a step toward me, but I stopped him. "Did you miss the part where I told you I regretted it?"

"Shit, Mila, we both know you didn't mean that."

"You know, you and I need to have a real conversation. You can't keep overshadowing everything with sex."

"While I agree with what you're saying, you are standing bare besides that lace thong, and I can't think about anything other than burying myself inside you," he growled as he closed the distance between us. He grabbed my hand and shoved it down his pants, where I could feel he was fully erect. "You do this to me with just the thought of your body beneath mine, not to mention seeing you here like this. I want you so bad, bella," he breathed.

My skin prickled with desire as I saw the need in his gorgeous honey-colored eyes and heard it in his voice. Against everything screaming in my head to walk away, my body betrayed me yet again. I stared into his eyes and slid my hand up and down his hard shaft. His eyes closed as he took a deep breath, letting out a low moan from his throat. When he looked back at me, his pupils were large, and his eyes hooded.

"I need you, Mila," he groaned as he gently pressed me against the cold mirror.

He cupped both of my breasts and kissed me passionately. It was very different than before. Even though he was tight with need, he kissed me with a gentleness that I had yet to experience. In that moment, I realized I didn't want gentle. I unbuckled his belt and unfastened his pants to have better access to him. When I pulled him free from his boxers, he ended our kiss to watch my hand slide up and down his big cock. My hand looked so tiny and could barely close around his thickness.

"I want you to fuck me," I whispered up at him, pulling his lips back to mine.

His gentleness ended when he moved his hands to my ass and dug his fingers into my flesh. I stroked him faster as he put a hand to my sex and started moving his hand in a fast, circular motion. I knew he could feel I was already wet through the fabric.

Without a word, he broke our kiss and turned me to face the mirror, making me let go of him. He watched me in the reflection as he slid his hand into the front of my panties and buried two fingers deep inside me, making me let out a moan. He quickly covered my mouth with his free hand.

"Gotta be quiet, Mila. I don't want to be interrupted," he growled in my ear.

I watched him in the mirror and felt him move my thong to the side, and with the wetness from his fingers, he rubbed it over the head of his cock. He pulled my waist away from the mirror slightly so that I was at a better angle, then locked eyes with mine in the reflection as he swiftly entered me. I opened my mouth to let out a moan, but he covered it in time. He smiled as he started to pump in and out of me, and I braced myself against the wall with my hands, turned on with watching each other through the mirror.

It didn't take long to get me close to coming.

"Almost there, bella," he breathed as he looked down to watch himself slide in and out of me from behind.

His hand tightened on my hip as he pumped faster, and I knew he was close. Almost simultaneously, we came undone, and I bit down on his hand in an attempt to keep quiet. I could feel him twitching inside me as my walls closed around him until we were both still, trying to get our breathing back to normal.

"You're so fucking amazing, Mila," he whispered in my ear. Then he kissed my back between my shoulder blades before carefully pulling out and putting himself back together.

I bent down to grab my bra, but when I turned to speak, he was gone. I stood stunned with my bra straps halfway up my arms when my phone pinged. I looked to see a message from George asking where I was. When I looked at the time, I cursed as I realized I was late for our meeting.

I was pissed I had let Marcello in yet again only for

him to just leave. We needed to talk, but he was making me feel more and more like a toy that he thought he could play with whenever he wanted, then toss aside when he was done. I refused to be used like that, and I would tell him as much as soon as I was done with my meeting. He would not be getting in my way any longer, nor would he be getting into my panties.

I rushed to the address George sent, flushed and flustered from my encounter with Marc. I was upset at him, but at the same time, thoroughly fucked and satisfied, making everything so damn confusing.

"Are you okay?" George asked as I rushed through the front door of the new space.

I looked around and realized we were in a large, unfinished area within a line of businesses within one building. I only saw two other doors and assumed one led to a bathroom and the other to a back exit or some kind of storage. I would have to explore later.

"Yea, I'm fine. I just ran over here. Sorry I'm late. My sister had me trying on dresses..." I rambled but realized I didn't need to explain myself. "You know what, it doesn't matter. Sorry I'm late."

I sat at the wooden folding table with George and tried to catch my breath. He poured a glass of water from a pitcher that was on the table and passed it to me. As I took a drink, I noticed his half-eaten sandwich and an open bag of chips in front of him. He was in his late forties and a shorter, pudgy guy. His hair was receding slightly, but his blue eyes were accented with long, black eyelashes, making him not too bad looking. There were times he seemed to get a little too comfortable with touching me, but he never crossed a line, so I let it be. Some people were just that way.

"How long have you been waiting?"

"Oh, I was already here taking care of some things," he shrugged.

I looked behind us again before turning back to George. "Will this be big enough for what we need? And how long will it take to renovate? We will have to actually build the studio area on top of needing a front office. This space looks a tad small."

"Don't fret, Mila. This will get us started. Once we get licensed and a few artists under our belts, we can build the studio you want. This will have to work for now." He winked at me and popped a chip into his mouth. "So, you mentioned you wanted to run something by me when I texted you about this place. What's on your mind?"

"I want us to resubmit our proposal to the board."

"Mila, we've been over this. Marcello DeLuca will not let it happen. He finds a way to interject every time. We have to find another way."

"Let me deal with Marcello DeLuca. I refuse to let him derail this any longer."

"It's not just DeLuca. The board consists of members related in one way or another to someone in the business. Most have deep connections not only with your family or his, but also with some of the other families that have always been in the background, yet seem to never fall out of the game. They are all looking for some semblance of control outside of your father, and they would get off on turning his little girl away."

"I will find a way to convince them. I'm not giving up. I'm not giving up. We just need to take a different approach. Maybe if we left you as a silent partner so that Marcello wouldn't be alerted to it, we could get it through and finally gain some traction."

George furrowed his brows at me as he considered what I said. He had never met my father face-to-face, but with him being aware of how he worked, I knew he was fearful of having to face my father at some point. So I had to convince him I had it under control and that if he confronted us about the business, I would take the blame, softening the blow for George. He had a right to fear my father, but I refused to let that fear keep me from my dreams.

"Okay," he finally gave in. He turned back to his meal and took a bite. "I'll make an appointment to sit with the board tomorrow."

"Thank you. Text me the time, and I will be there. Make sure our lawyer is also there with the contracts ready to be signed. I don't want anything to halt this any longer."

I went home with a new bounce in my step. I was finally going to get what I wanted, and this time, Marcello would not get in the way. If I was to be forced into this silly marriage, I would get something out of it. Of course, he wouldn't know that I would be gone before I walked down the aisle. I could make music anywhere, as long as I had full control of the new music label and all it entails. I was not giving up on my dream.

The next day, I picked out my favorite suit. It was beige in color and fit me perfectly. I paired it with matching pumps and a designer bag Anya got for me a few Christmases ago. I pulled my dark hair into a loose bun at the nape of my neck and had Harper help me with my makeup. I was dressed to impress, and confidence was oozing off of me.

"Go get 'em tiger," Harper said before smacking my ass as I left, making me squeal and let out a full-bellied laugh. I was happy and excited for the first time in days.

I met George and our lawyer at an office building

shared between the Fedorov's and the DeLuca's. I had hoped George would be able to keep our meeting quiet so that I wouldn't have to see Marcello. He hadn't shown up at any of the other meetings. Why would this one be different? I had my proposal in my bag and was ready to slay my presentation. The board heard it all twice before, but I had changed some points to make it more appealing. Before, it was George who had presented our proposal, so I was hoping that with me taking the lead, it would be a shoe-in. With the board being affiliated with my family and Marcello's, they would know who I was, and I hoped that gave me the extra power to produce a thumbs-up from every member.

"Here goes nothing, kiddo," George said as he led us into the elevator.

He let his hand rest on my lower back a little too long, making me feel uncomfortable, but he moved it when I turned slightly. I turned to our lawyer, Hunter Beckett, to counter the awkward silence. He was in his mid-thirties and had a great track record as a business lawyer. I had no doubt he would make sure everything was in place, legally. He also had no deep connections with the families, so he didn't have a hidden agenda. He had integrity and ensured to back up all of his clients, no matter who they were.

"Did George send you my new proposal so that you could draw up the necessary documents?"

"He did, and I have the new contracts here. All they need to do is sign, and you are good to go."

When we reached the top floor, George led us to the conference room where the board was already assembled. They were eight in total and a wide range of ages. I was not familiar with any of them, so I had no idea who had connections with which family. There was an older gentleman, who looked to be older than my father, sitting at the head of the large, oval table. I couldn't get a read from his stone-faced demeanor, but I imagined he was not happy to be in yet another meeting about a music label.

To his right sat a blonde woman, who appeared to be in her mid-thirties. She had make-up to match that of a glamour model with a tightly fitted red dress and seemed very out of place. Beside her were two more men who offered small smiles to us as we entered, both of whom seemed to be around my father's age.

On the opposite side was a guy that was my age and an arrogant mother fucker. You know how sometimes it just wafts off of people and they don't even have to open their mouths to know they are smug, arrogant assholes? That was this guy. There was an older woman next to him who looked like she could be a touch older than my father and had short, wavy grey hair. Then there were two more men next to her, who resembled the two across from them. I wondered if the four of them were related but quickly let it go.

"Good morning, Miss Fedorov," the older woman greeted me as I walked in.

Everyone stood until I took my seat at the opposite end of the table, then they all sat back down. George and Mr. Beckett took their seats on either side of me.

"Good morning, everyone," I said as I removed my documents from my bag, then I passed out a copy to each board member and shared my copy with George. He already knew what was in it, but I offered it so that he could keep up with the presentation. "I have before you the proposal for Mila Music Industries."

"Miss Fedorov, we have already heard the proposal from Mr. Martin for this and have turned it down every time. What makes you think this time will be any different?" the man sitting at the head of the table asked. His annoyance at being present for the meeting was obvious, and he didn't care.

"As you flip through the pages, you will see a new trajectory with new numbers in profits and artists. And with all due respect, you have yet to offer me a solid answer as to why you have turned down my proposals in the past. I am taking full control of this company, with Mr. Martin only being a silent investor. There should be no reason to turn this down with the obvious benefits and profits I have shown in this proposal."

"Mila, we have given sufficient reason-" the woman in red started, but I cut her off.

"Which are bullshit, if I can be frank. My business would be small enough but also has the potential to bring in strong revenue and corner a new market. There's no reason to deny this proposal. My lawyer even has everything drawn up. All you need to do is sign on the dotted line."

The door suddenly opened, and in walked Marcello and one of his men. The room erupted in hushed talk among the board members as I stared at Marc, who was staring back at me.

"Here we go," George muttered under his breath, but I heard him.

There was no way Marcello was going to waltz in here and steamroll my meeting. No way in fucking hell.

CHAPTER
FIVE
MARCELLO

I WAS in the middle of a meeting with a new tech company about an app they need backing for when Shane called me. He knew to only call if it was important, so I halted the meeting and moved to the hall to take the call.

"What is it, Shane? I'm in the middle of a meeting," I cut through my teeth.

"Boss, you're gonna want to hear this," Shane answered convincingly.

"Out with it, then."

"I just followed Mila to the offices on West Eighth Street."

"That's our main office with the Fedorov's. What is she doing there?"

"I don't know, but she met with a lawyer and that guy, George Martin."

My blood boiled the moment I heard the name. George was a piece of scum I had been trying to scrub away for over two years. To hear he was with Mila made me even more pissed off. She had no idea who she was getting into business with.

"How do you know they were with a lawyer?"

"I recognized him from billboards, and he's been used by some of our associates," Shane answered.

"Fuck."

I quickly closed off the meeting, promising them we would reschedule, and high-tailed it across town to Mila's location. I couldn't for the life of me understand why she would work with that piece of shit. Had she asked her father about George, she would know to stay far away. He never dealt with him personally, but he was aware of my issue with him through my father. He was on our radar to make sure he was blocked on all fronts. I had connections in the state department and had managed to block his licensing in the past, which would make it impossible for him to legitimize his business. So it pissed me off even more that he tried to work around it by using Mila, knowing she would be recognized with the board. The dirty scum probably assumed they would never think to deny the Don's daughter. It was the only scenario I could come up with as to why she would be in cahoots with him.

When I got there, Shane was waiting for me at the front door.

"What floor?"

"Top," he answered.

"Fuck. Why is she meeting with the board?"

"No idea, boss. I called you the second I saw where they were going."

I didn't even fuck with the elevator. I took the stairs, two at a time, with Shane trailing me. I stormed to the conference room and walked right in. The moment I saw Mila, I stared her down.

"What are you doing here?" she asked angrily.

"Everyone, out!" I boomed, never taking my eyes off her.

Everyone hurried out, but George and their lawyer stayed behind, standing next to Mila as though to protect her. *How cute*! When they didn't move to leave, I walked right up to George, towering over him and stared down at him with a look of murder in my eyes. I watched the pudgy guy balk and swallow hard before offering an apology to Mila and scurrying out, their lawyer on his heels, slamming the door behind them.

I faced Mila as she squared her shoulders and folded her arms in front of her in defiance. I admired her gumption.

"What the fuck, Marc?"

"Leave everything here. We are leaving, now."

"Screw you. I will not leave here until they sign off on this deal. I'm sick of you sticking your nose where it doesn't belong. If you expect me to walk down that aisle, you will stop getting in my way."

"I'm sorry, bella. I can't let you do this."

"You don't get to control my life," she snapped. I could tell she was hurting, but I knew she would crash and burn getting into business with George Martin.

"Not your life, Mila. But this, I have full control over. I know you don't understand, but you will soon."

"This is so fucked," she bit out.

"Come have lunch with me," I offered to change the subject. I didn't want to divulge all the information yet, so I hoped I could distract her another way.

"No."

"Mila, I know you're upset. Let me make it up to you. Maybe in a few months, we can re-evaluate this proposal." I grabbed a folder left behind by George and the lawyer and held out my hand for Mila to take. I watched her face go through multiple expressions as she contemplated leaving with me. Finally, she took my hand, making me let out the breath I didn't know I was holding when I turned to lead her away from the conference room.

I told Shane, who was waiting in the hall, that he was driving. Mila followed quietly, not taking her hand back. Once we were in the car, Shane asked where we were headed.

"To my place," I answered, and Mila turned to me with a scowl.

"You said lunch."

"Easy, bella. I want to show you something first, then we will eat."

She huffed as she turned toward the window, away from me, and watched the scenery pass by. I took the moment to look over her proposal, impressed with what she had put together. I had no idea she was connected to the music company George had been trying to start. Her name was left off the documents in the past. Now, it was all in her name, showing George as a silent investor.

At first, I just wanted to get Mila alone, but realizing she was serious enough about music to start her own record label, I wanted to show her my musical instruments back home. My family wasn't the musical type, other than my mother. When I was younger, I would sit and listen to her playing her cello and beg for her to teach me what she knew. As I grew older, she first taught me how to read music and then how to play the cello. I taught myself how to play the guitar and piano, but only the basics. I collected instruments that were antiques or with the thought of learning to play them here and there. But, instead, they now acted as wall decorations on my office wall in my suite. When my mother passed away, I was often told to leave it alone and that it had no place in my life. Eventually, I just left it alone, being so caught up in my father's business. I would play from time to time, but my love for music had died with my mother.

When we got to my place above the bar where I met my future wife, I took Mila's bag from her and set it on the couch. I laid her folder next to it, so she knew I wasn't taking it. She didn't need to know I would get a copy anyway.

"I want to show you something that means a lot to me," I said calmly as I walked to the study just left of the entrance.

Mila followed me hesitantly but gasped when she saw the wall lined with musical instruments. On one side of my office was floor-to-ceiling bookcases, but the opposite wall housed instruments ranging from a small piano to a cello in the corner. I walked to the cello, took it from its stand, and walked it over to Mila.

"This was my mother's. It was her favorite instrument, and she used to play for us as we sat in the lounge and wound down for the evening. It's one of my favorite sounds."

"It's beautiful," Mila breathed as she let her fingers roam over the strings and wood. "Do you mind if I play it?"

"I would love that," I answered. I had no idea she knew how to play and was excited at the chance to hear it again.

She sat in one of the leather chairs in the middle of the room, and I sat opposite her. Without hesitation, she started playing a number I recognized as Bach's Cello Suite No. 1, which was an advanced piece.

I leaned back in the chair and watched in awe as her fingers moved expertly over the strings with the bow moving seamlessly. I closed my eyes as the music filled the room. It felt as though my mother was with me again, and my heart swelled. My throat grew thick as tears threatened to fall, but I refused to let them free. Blinking them back, I opened my eyes and sat straighter, covering my mouth with a hand so that she couldn't see my expression well. When she was done, I just stared at her in silence, partly because I didn't fucking know what to say.

"Was that not okay?" she finally asked, and it killed me that she questioned her talent, but even more that I made her do so.

"I am blown away, bella. It was as if my mother was here again."

She smiled sweetly at me but then suddenly appeared nervous. She returned the cello back to its place and stood in front of me.

"Let me have my company."

"No," I answered matter-of-factly.

"For Christ's sake, Marcello. Why are you doing this? How does it hurt you for me to see this through?"

"It doesn't."

She stood in frustration, shaking her head at me. She sucked her lips in, looking over my shoulder in thought. I knew she wanted to tear me a new one. It was hot to see her so pissed and fighting for what she wanted. I wished I could give it to her, but I just couldn't do it. She looked back at me, her beautiful emerald eyes hard and cold.

"You can't control my life, Marcello."

I hated it when she used my full name. For some reason, her using the shortened version felt more intimate. I stood, only inches away from her, and trailed my thumb along her full bottom lip. She didn't flinch at my touch, even though she was upset at me.

"You're *mine*, bella. And so is your life once we say our vows in less than two weeks."

I didn't give her a chance to respond. Instead, I kissed her passionately, the emotions of her playing my mother's cello still flowing through me. I pulled her tighter, and she didn't resist. Instead, she melted in my arms and opened her mouth for our tongues to dance.

I backed her to her chair, and she sat down with a plop, but we didn't disconnect. Then I leaned down over her, resting my hands on the arms of the chair. She was pissing me off by being so defiant, but at the same time, I admired her fighting for what she wanted. Still, I needed her to realize that I would be the one in control of the relationship, in and out of the bedroom.

She reached her hands up around my neck, trying to pull me down to get closer, but I remained where I stood. Instead, I moved a hand between her legs and rubbed her where I knew she wanted to feel my touch. She moaned into our kiss as I worked her in circles and opened her legs for more friction against the fabric.

"Please," she begged when she finally pulled away from my lips.

"Please what, bella?" I breathed.

"I want you," she moaned.

"How badly do you want me?"

I moved my hand faster, adding more pressure through her pants. She looked sexy as hell in the suit she was wearing. Her pink, plump lips were raw from my kisses, and her head was leaning back against the chair, her eyes closed. It was a sight to behold as she ground her hips against my hand, searching for a release. It was a shame I wouldn't see it through, but I needed to make a point.

As soon as I knew she was at the brink, I removed my hand and stood straight. When she opened her eyes and looked at me in confusion, desperate for my touch, I almost didn't go through with it. But I turned and started to walk away.

"What are you doing?" she called after me.

"I have a meeting to get to. You can see yourself out," I called back to her as I left her alone in the office of my suite, wanting and unsatisfied.

CHAPTER
SIX
MILA

I SLAMMED the door to my apartment and threw my bag on the couch, plopping down next to it.

"Ugh!" I yelled loudly before dropping my face into my hands.

How could I be such an idiot? Not only did I fail to convince Marcello to let me have my music business, but I also allowed him to seduce me yet again. Then the bastard left me hanging, panting like an animal. I was mortified that I couldn't seem to control myself when it came to him. No matter how much he pisses me off and how determined I am to get away from it all, he pulls me in with one sultry look or a touch that burns a fire through my veins every time.

It made it worse that I had thought I saw a shift in him when I played his mother's cello. When he first presented it to me, I had the split-second thought that my playing it could help tip his decision in my favor when it came to my music label, playing on his emotional attachment to it. But the moment I started to play, I got lost in the beautiful music. I watched Marcello's demeanor relax completely, and a hint of emotions flashed through his expression. It was the first time I had seen both love and hurt in his eyes. Even his kiss was more passionate, with an undertone of need outside of lust. Stronger. It took me a moment to realize he had truly left me alone in his suite, so close to on orgasm, filled with need for him. What kind of asshole does that? How could I be so naïve to think he could actually have feelings for me? Once again, I felt like his plaything.

"What's got you steamin'?" Harper asked, pulling her T-shirt on as she walked over to the couch. "Oh no, did they deny you again?"

"They didn't get a chance to make a decision. Marcello barged in and interrupted the meeting, made everyone scatter, and told me he wouldn't allow it to happen."

"What the hell? How did he even know about it?"

"I don't even know," I huffed as I leaned back and stared at the ceiling.

Jacob walked out of Harper's bedroom and sat on the arm of the couch next to her.

"Thanks for keepin' it in your bedroom this time," I said dryly.

"Shut it," Harper laughed as she shoved my arm lightly. "So, what are you going to do about Marcello?"

"Throw him off a cliff."

"Well, I'm glad you're tapping into your roots with that idea," Harper teased. "But I think we should think of a less murdery approach."

"The more and more I just want to get out of here. Maybe once I'm in New York, I will have better luck. I can start over."

"When are you going to New York?" Jacob asked.

My heart started to race, and I looked over at

Harper with my eyes wide. I had forgotten he was here and silently cussed at myself for letting it slip.

"It's fine," Harper insisted. "He won't tell anyone, right snookie-poo?" She turned and flashed her boyfriend an over-exaggerated smile as she batted her eyelashes at him.

"Your secrets are safe with me," Jacob agreed.

My heart rate slowed slightly, but I still felt a little worried. For some reason, my body was trying to warn me to be cautious while my brain couldn't come up with a good reason why. I chalked it up to my stress and brushed it off.

"I'm leaving before our vows are final," I answered Jacob's question. His eyebrows raised in alarm at my answer.

"How will you manage to do that? Won't Marcello, and your father, just track you down?" he asked.

I looked back at my friend with a scowl. As far as I knew, Jacob didn't know who I was or who I was marrying. Harper also told me she understood the importance of no one else knowing my plan. I couldn't risk it not working and to be forced to marry Marcello. Harper hissed with a sharp intake of breath.

"Sorry. I kind of explained everything to him," she said carefully. "You know how pillow talk can be," she shrugged.

"No, Harper. I actually don't know. This isn't shit we just loosely talk about with whoever we decide to sleep with," I snapped at her.

I instantly felt like an asshole. She had been with Jacob for about four months, and I knew he meant a lot to her. I was already pissed off at Marcello, and hearing that she was telling my secrets to someone when she knows not to just made my temper worse.

"That was harsh, Mila," Harper said gently. She had

every right to be upset with me, but she could see I was already stressed. It always impressed me that she could read me and respond with understanding, unlike me, who just responds with a burst of emotion. I knew my stubbornness and temper got me into some binds, but it was in my DNA, thanks to my Russian roots and the Don being my father. "He can help us get out of here."

I locked eyes with Jacob, hoping he could see the seriousness on my face. "You cannot tell a single soul, Jake. I'm dead serious."

He placed his hand on his chest above his heart. "You can trust me, I swear. I want to help. No one should be forced to marry someone against their will. Just tell me how I can help."

I looked him over for a moment. There was still some lingering doubt, but I decided to push it aside and trust him. I nodded silently to show I accepted his offer.

"So, what's the plan?" Harper asked.

"I think it would be best to wait for as long as possible. It may be too risky to leave on the day of the wedding, so the night before would be perfect. We would have to wait until late, when everyone is sleeping and expects me to be asleep."

"How are you going to get very far without your father being on your tail?" Jacob asked.

"I have someone who could get us new identities and documents."

"You only have a little over a week to get that done. Will there be enough time?" Harper asked.

"This guy is a genius, and he's fast. Especially with a little incentive."

"Incentive?"

"Money, obviously," I chuckled.

"You refuse to touch the money your parents have

put into your account. Won't it be suspicious if you suddenly take some out?" Harper asked.

She knew I hated to have connections with my father's money. I knew he had legitimate partnerships and businesses, but there was also the chance of it being dirty money, and I never wanted any part of it.

"My grandmother sent me some cash as a gift when I graduated college. I never put it in the bank, so my father would have no way of tracking it."

"She wouldn't tell him or your mom?"

"She may be an elder who understands that world, but she also understands my side of things and how controlling my father is. She wanted me to have my own money without someone else ordering me how to use it."

"Why haven't you used that to open your business then? Why do you need that George guy?" Harper asked.

"He has more than ten years of experience in the music industry and has connections. Plus, it would be too suspicious for me to have the money for that but not touch any of the money in my account. I won't throw my grandmother under the bus like that."

"Then the first thing we gotta do is get a hold of your guy for the documents," Jacob chimed in. "Once we have that secured, we can get you out. I'll drive you all the way to New York and make sure you guys get settled."

"You could stay with us," Harper said sweetly to Jacob. He just smiled and leaned down to peck her on the lips. It was adorable, although he never answered.

"Think you can play the part of a bride-to-be long enough to not alert anyone that you're having second thoughts?" Harper asked.

"They would suspect something is off if I didn't

kick and scream the whole way, so it will be a piece of cake," I joked.

"Ok, so Mila is getting you guys new documents," Jacob finalized our plan. "Harper, you can get things ready to pack quickly and leave the night before the wedding. I will plan the escape route and make sure we can make it to New York without detection."

Harper squealed and clapped her hands. "This is so exciting!"

"Remember there is danger in doing this, Harper," I warned.

"That makes it all the more exciting!"

The next day, I mindlessly followed Anya from shop to shop, picking out accessories for my wedding as well as outfits for our honeymoon. I was uncomfortable with the amount of lingerie she picked out and with how little fabric there was for each outfit.

"Is it really necessary to have these, Anya? I mean, look at them. I could just walk around naked and save you some money," I snorted, holding up a tiny piece of black lace to make my point.

"Trust me, Mila. Guys go crazy for this shit."

"I'm sure they do, when they are both deeply in love and wanting to turn one another on. You know, like in a *normal* marriage."

"Enough, Mila. We are all aware you aren't happy with this marriage. But the truth of it is that you can't get out of it, so why not make the best of it? Marcello is not as bad as he seems. You may come to find that there is a chance for you two to fall in love if you just gave it a chance." I gave my sister an annoyed look, letting her feel the doubt roll off of me. "Besides, if his personality can't win you over, his skills in the sheets might," she giggled.

There it was, the feeling of my lunch coming back up. I almost forgot that my sister dated Marcello when they were in high school, making me despise my situation even more. The way he had looked at her during our family dinner made me wonder if he still loved her. It felt wrong to not only sleep with my sister's ex, but even worse to marry him. Then, on top of that, I could feel myself falling for him despite my best efforts to turn my feelings off. Even after he humiliated me by leaving me hanging in his suite, I could still feel the pull toward him. I wanted to hate him, but I just couldn't.

"That's easy for you to say. You got out of it when you married Camden. You are the reason this is being forced on me. Don't you feel a little terrible?"

"Survival of the fittest, sissy," Anya said a touch too chipperly and walked to search for more lingerie.

It hurt that she seemed to not care that she was helping to send me to my personal hell. She had gotten the life she wanted, which was why she was so chipper to plan my wedding, happy it was me and not her.

I let my eyes roam over the tables full of bras and panties. There was one particular pair that really stood out to me. The bra was red lace with a beautiful pattern that would just barely cover my nipples, and the matching panties had a soft, silk thong with the same beautiful design on the front. I imagined prancing around Marc's suite in it, the light from the large, floor-to-ceiling windows acting as my spotlight.

I quickly developed an idea of how to get back at him for his little game of leaving me hanging, and these would offer the perfect bait. I would make sure I got him back before I left him forever. I wanted his last memory of me to be when I had him so hard and wanting me, then watching me walk away from him, bare ass and all.

"Come on, let's go pay for these then grab lunch," Anya said breaking me out of my thoughts. I grabbed the red lace bra and panties and followed my sister to the register, scoffing at the price on display. "Don't worry, Daddy's paying for it," she snickered.

The family car was waiting for us at the curb, and Anya threw my new bags into the trunk with ten others from our day of shopping. Instead of getting in the car, she headed down the street to a café on the corner. She chose a corner booth and ordered us both salads and water.

"What if I wanted a burger?" I challenged her.

"Oh, please. Your wedding is in a week. You need to make sure you'll fit into your dress."

"Do you mean to be so bitchy, or can you just not gauge your rudeness?" I asked her with equal parts sarcasm and truth.

"I was thinking lilies for your bouquet and center-pieces," she continued as though I had never spoken, scrolling through something on her phone. "Do you have a song in mind for your first dance?"

"Is there a song called kill me now?" I deadpanned.

Anya slowly raised her eyes to glare at me. "Make some kind of effort, Mila."

"Whatever song you pick, I'm sure it will be fine."

"I realize this is torture for you. But a lot can happen in a week. You never know how you will feel. Then, if you go out onto that dance floor for your first dance with a man you actually love to a song that means nothing, you will be kicking yourself."

I remained quiet as she turned her attention back to her phone. I wanted to tell her she was crazy if she thought I would fall for Marcello in just a week, but I couldn't. I was already having strong feelings toward him, despite my desperation to run away. I felt a lump forming in my throat, threatening to bring tears with it, but I pushed it down. For a moment, I let the thought of walking down the aisle to Marc standing at the other end with a look of unconditional love and adoration into my head. I allowed myself to feel the love, excitement, and safety, but only briefly before shoving them away. I just as quickly remembered how he treated me like a toy. Like he could control my life and stand in the way of my dreams.

I was done with men trying to control me and my life. Both my father and my future husband stood in the way of me living a life I wanted for myself. I'd spent twenty-two years waiting for the day I could get out of my father's control, only to be handed to someone else just as controlling for the remainder of my life. I would not give in. I would leave for New York before our wedding day and never look back.

CHAPTER
SEVEN
MARCELLO

MILA HAD INVADED my mind since I left her at my suite. I was sure she would call to cuss me out, but she never did. She didn't even send a text, leaving me a little disappointed. I knew she would be pissed about what I had done, but I also thought it would in turn make her want me more, like in a cat and mouse game. Clearly, I misjudged how she would respond since two days had passed, and I hadn't heard from her. I was actually worried I had pushed her too far and was uncomfortable with the feeling that I might have hurt her in some way — very new emotions I wasn't ready for, but Mila somehow burrowed her way through the walls I had spent years building.

I had to attend a business meeting but could hardly focus on the discussion, with Mila taking up every inch of my thoughts, and I couldn't wait for it to be over. When I was finally free, I was in desperate need of clearing my head. I needed to understand how I felt about my future wife and figure out how to proceed. I needed her to see me in a different light. For her to see me trying to be a good partner instead of the player she might have heard about. For her to get to know who I truly was instead of the persona I had to portray for business. I smiled as Shane pulled up to the curb of the restaurant on my Ducati motorcycle.

"Here ya go, boss," he said as he dismounted and handed me my helmet and gloves. I handed him my car keys in exchange.

"Thanks for bringing her to me. I need to take a ride, clear my head."

"Want me to follow at a distance? Word of your marriage is getting around. Never know who will come out of the woodwork."

"No, I'll be fine. I hardly ever get this beauty out," I said as I sat on my bike and patted the metal in front of me. "No one would think to look for me on this, so I'm not worried."

"Whatever you say. I'll head back to the house then."

I nodded at Shane, put on my helmet, and took off. I wanted to get to the hills where there was an open road and I could really open her up. I loved to feel the speed and power under my control. The cool air gliding around me added a feeling of flying that I could never get enough of. The sun had set, and the clear, dark sky showed off its bright stars. It was a perfect night for a ride.

As I soared over the hills and around the bends, I thought of the curve of Mila's hips, then her full perfect tits. I thought about how innocent and sweet she had looked at me after playing my mother's cello and the way I felt electricity passing between us when we kissed. The way her smile made my heart swell in a way that I was too embarrassed to admit.

I was rounding a large curve when a black van suddenly pulled out in front of me. I felt my breath hitch as I had to make a split-second decision that seemed to pass by in slow motion. I could stay on my bike, hold on tight, and hope for the best when I crashed into the side of the van, or I could lean over and bail, risking road rash. In that second, I chose the second option and bailed out before it was too late.

I gritted my teeth as I slid across the pavement, feeling my skin burn where the fabric tore open. I watched as my bike slammed into the van, fucking pissed that it was ruined. I was ready to get up and tear the driver a new asshole when the side door slid open and two masked men hopped out. Then, the driver got out with a black bag and large white zip ties in his hand. *Fuck, this is not happening.*

Before I could say a word, the two men grabbed my arms as the driver approached and threw the bag over my head. I tried fighting myself free from their grasp, but I was too sore from skidding across the pavement. They managed to bind my wrists with the zip ties, and then tossed me into the van.

"Who the fuck are you dip-shits? Do you have any idea who you're fucking with?" I seethed, pissed that I had sent Shane away. My arrogance had really got me into some shit this time.

"Shut the fuck up," a voice ground out before I felt a sharp pain in my head and fell into blackness.

My head throbbed as I started to come to. I was breathing hot hair, with the bag still over my head, sweat falling down from my hairline. I groaned as my stiff sore body began to wake up, and I realized I was in a hard chair, my hands bound behind me. There was a faint smell of pizza and cigarette smoke mixed with a hint of perfume that was vaguely familiar but very out of place. I tried to test my restraints to see if they were weak enough to break free from them, but I stopped moving when I heard heavy footsteps approaching.

Suddenly, the bag was pulled off my head. I instantly took in my surroundings, realizing I was sitting in a grubby motel room. I looked to the man sitting on the edge of a bed in front of me.

"What the fuck is this, Bruno?" I snapped. "Untie me right now. You know good and well what the fuck will happen to you for this."

Bruno Vasquez was the big brother of Bianca, whom I had dated off and on when I got bored. We had never gotten serious, and she had always voiced how she would tie me down and marry me some day. Never would I have taken her at her word to pull something like this off. They were also a family with close ties to mine, but were always causing more trouble than they were worth. My father had been discussing cutting their whole clan loose.

"Ahh," he brushed my comment aside. "They know we play. I'll just tell your dad we were playing a harmless prank."

Bruno stood at six feet tall with black, oil-slicked hair. His eyes were just as dark, and his crooked grin was accented with a gold tooth in the front. He always embodied the essence of a jabroni and dressed the part perfectly, thick gold chains and all.

"My bike and clothes say otherwise."

"Eh, you guys got money, yeah? You can just buy a new one," Bruno chuckled.

Two more guys who I recognized as friends of Bruno's walked in. They must have been the ones to help throw me in the van.

"We've had him for long enough, Bruno. Get to the

point so that we can get outta here before his brothers find us," one of them warned.

"Stop your worryin'. We'll be long gone before anyone knows he's missing'."

"It's been over an hour. You're cutting it close."

Over an hour? They must have drugged me after they knocked me out.

"What is this about, Bruno? And are the restraints necessary?" I tried to see if I could get him to free me. I wanted to punch the little prick right in the nose.

"I think you know why the restraints are necessary, my man. And we are here on behalf of Bianca," Bruno answered. I let my head fall back and let out a guttural laugh. "What's so funny, DeLuca?"

"That you think this little show of false power would get me to marry your sister. All it's going to do is make you all look like idiots, and my father will no longer have anything to do with you. He will make sure no one throughout the entire state will work with any of you. You've sealed your fate here, Bruno."

"Nah, man. Your father will want you back, so I figure I could ask for a hefty ransom. You know, just in case he does turn his back on us."

"You're an idiot."

Bruno scowled at me, then stood and clocked me across my jaw. I spit out a little blood, then stared at him like a mad man. He knew better than to touch a DeLuca and was out of his mind if he thought he was untouchable just because I was momentarily restrained.

I was about to make an attempt to break the rickety wooden chair I was sitting in when the door was busted open.

— ∽⟲∾ —

Mila

It was half past nine, and I was lounging on my couch in sweats, ready for bed. I had decided to watch a little television to tire me out. As I flipped through the channels, I stopped when I saw images of Marcello, then of me. *What the hell?* I turned the volume up a little to hear what the reporter was saying and realized it was an entertainment conglomerate, covering the details of our wedding. Annoyed that it was now blasted to the public, I brought up the guide to find a movie to rent instead. I finally landed on a favorite and settled in to watch when my door opened abruptly. I knew Harper had just left for work and thought I had the door locked. In alarm, I shot up to my feet to come face to face with Marcello's brother, Dante.

"What are you doing?" I demanded.

"Get your bag and shoes. You need to come with me," he ordered.

I crossed my arms in front of me and didn't move an inch, staring at him in defiance.

"Now, Mila!" he yelled.

"Who do you think you are, barging in here and ordering-" my voice hitched to a high note as Dante moved forward and tossed me over his shoulder. "Put me down, you neanderthal!"

"I told you come with me, you didn't listen. Here we are."

He grabbed my bag and keys from the table next to the door and walked out of my apartment with me slung over his shoulder. Then he stopped to lock the door and rushed down the steps and out to a black Range Rover waiting in front of the building. The SUV door was opened, and I was unceremoniously thrown into the back seat, the door slamming behind me. As I righted myself to a sitting position, I saw a guy around the same age as Dante sliding into the driver's seat and Dante into the passenger seat. As soon as he was seated, he tossed my bag back to me.

"What's going on? Why are you dragging me out of my apartment at eleven o'clock at night?"

"Marcello's missing."

My stomach dropped, and my mouth hung open as I tried to register what Dante had just told me. "I'm sorry, what?"

"He's missing. We don't know who has him or why, so we need to make sure you are safe. Our father wanted me to come get you so that he can be the one to ensure your safety."

"Why would anyone be dumb enough to take Marc? How long has he been missing?"

"He went for a ride after a business dinner earlier tonight," the driver answered. "He should have been back home over an hour ago."

"I'm sorry, what's your name again?"

"Shane."

"Okay, Shane. What makes you think he's missing? It's only been an hour or two. He probably stopped off for a drink or something. This doesn't sound alarming at all."

"Marcello is meticulous and hardly ever moves without letting me know. If he decided to go out for drinks, he would've told me. Especially with your wedding being so public. We worried someone would try something, but he didn't believe he was in danger." Shane hit the steering wheel. "Shit! I should have gone with my gut and followed his ass into the hills."

"Cristiano and Dominic are looking for him now. Luckily, we put a tracker on his Ducati when he first got it. They think they have found his location," Dante said without looking back. His voice was deep and a matter of fact.

I sat back in my seat and watched the lights fly by as Shane drove us to who knows where. My heart had sped up as I started thinking about what could happen to Marc if he had really been kidnapped. I worried my fingers together, realizing I didn't want anything bad to happen to him. Sure, he pissed me off, and I hated that I was being forced to marry him, but I had to admit that I was falling for him, and my current reaction was proof.

We pulled into a house similar to my father's, only this one was on the water and had more of a modern industrial look to it. Shane pulled the car to the front and parked. Dante got out and opened my door for me as Shane headed to open the front door to the house.

"Whose place is this?" I asked Dante as he led me to the door Shane was holding open.

"It's our father's."

I followed the men into the back of the house, where floor-to-ceiling windows looked out to the Pacific. There was a large fireplace surrounded by stone and stark white couches around a concrete coffee table. In the living room sat Antonio DeLuca, a few of his men, and my father. *Shit, why is he here?*

When the patriarchs realized Dante and Shane were back, they both rose from their seats and looked to me.

"Mila, I am happy to see you're alright," Marcello's father cooed as he walked over and kissed me on the cheek. My father remained standing, staring at me emotionlessly.

"Have you heard anything from the boys tracking his location?" I asked as I was led to the couch and sat down. Shane brought me a hot cup of tea.

"They just got word to us that they tracked his bike

to an old, rundown motel. They are going to let us know what they find," Marcello's father said. "I'm sure he's fine, but we needed to make sure you were safe."

"Thanks," I said quietly before taking a sip of my tea. I looked at my father, who had moved to watch the flames in the fireplace. I still didn't understand why he was there, but I knew better not to ask.

"I should be the one out there looking for him!" I heard Shane yelling at Dante, who was shushing him and trying to keep him calm.

I looked around and noticed everyone was on edge. Even though Mr. DeLuca put on a brave, calm face, I could feel the stress radiating from him. His shoulders were taught as he spoke to his men in hushed tones. Not knowing what to do, I busied myself stirring my tea. My thoughts wandered to Marc and the way he made me feel. It wasn't the anger or the annoyance — it was the passion, the fire. The way he made me feel worshiped every time we were alone. That invisible pull that I know we both felt, no matter how much we wanted to deny it. I started thinking about how our life could be if we were able to take time to learn about one another. I felt my chest swell with the feelings of love for the man I was determined to run away from. *Would I be able to leave? Was I kidding myself thinking I would just be able to walk away without looking back?*

Suddenly, we heard the heavy front door hit the wall as it was pushed open and the sounds of feet scuffling across the floor. Everyone turned their attention to the noise. I set my cup down and stood, wondering what we would see.

In walked Dominic and Cristiano with a beaten and bloody Marcello. They were each side of him, helping him stay on his feet. The sight of him broke down my walls of stoicism, and tears streamed down my face.

"Jesus, man," Shane gushed as he walked up and hugged Marcello, not worrying about the obvious pain his friend was in. He stood back and looked Marc in the face, resting his hands on his shoulders. "What happened?"

"Give him some room, Shane," Antonio ordered as he moved closer to take in the sight of his son. I peeked behind me to see that my father didn't move from his spot and just watched with his hands in his pockets.

"We need to get him cleaned up. It looks like he's got some nasty road rash," Dominic said as they continued to move Marc into the living room.

I tried to wipe my tears away before he could see me but failed. Marc's eyes locked onto mine, and his face changed from pain to concern. How could this man be concerned with me when he was obviously hurt? More tears streamed down my face when I got a better look at his torn clothing and the blood that was stained on the fabric. A large bruise was also starting to form on his face. I wanted to go to him. To hug him and do my damnedest to help him feel better. I even thought I saw him start moving toward me, but his brothers redirected him into another part of the house to get him cleaned up.

"Come on, Mila. Marcello is fine. It's time you went home," my father said from behind me, making me jump. I hadn't heard him approaching.

"I want to wait to make sure he really is okay," I protested.

"He will need to rest, and it's rude to stay where you're of no use. He will come to you if he wants to see you."

"But-" I started again but he cut me off.

"Do as you're told, Mila."

The Don signaled one of the men over and told him to make sure I got home alright and that there was no one suspicious lurking around. He didn't leave any room for me to argue, and I was forced out to the car and to leave Marc behind. It broke my heart to not be there for him, solidifying the truth that I was, in fact, falling in love with Marcello DeLuca.

CHAPTER
EIGHT

MILA

I COULD HARDLY SLEEP all night. I wanted to make sure Marcello was okay, but my overbearing father had refused to let me stay. I couldn't even get through to his phone, it just went to voicemail. So, I sat on my couch with a cup of coffee, staring at the wall, waiting to hear from him when Harper walked in.

"Damn, Mila. You look like shit," she announced.

"Gee, thanks," I deadpanned.

She plopped down next to me, staring at me as she waited for me to explain my current condition. When I just sipped my coffee, she gave in and asked, "What gives? You look like your cat died, only you don't have a cat."

"Marcello was taken last night," I answered.

"Holy shit. Is he alright?"

"I guess. His brother came and took me to their family home until they found Marcello. When they brought him in, he was beaten to hell and all bloody. It looked bad, Harper."

"Then why are you here instead of there with him?"

"My father forced me out of the house and made the DeLuca men bring me home," I responded angrily.

"Why would your dad even be there?"

"Who knows? To make sure Marcello was back and our wedding was still on track?"

"That's cold. I'm not sure I ever want to meet your dad," Harper teased as she rose from the couch. "I'm hopping in the shower. Do you need anything?"

"I'm good."

Not long after Harper left the room, my phone rang. I was so eager to grab it that I spilled hot coffee on my hand.

"Ouch, shit," I hissed as I grabbed my phone and saw it was Marc. My heart jumped into my throat before starting to race. I had to take a deep breath before answering. "How are you?"

"Good morning to you too, bella," Marcello's voice sailed through the receiver like honey.

"Fuck pleasantries. Tell me you're okay."

"Nothing that won't heal. I'll be as good as new in a couple of days."

"You need to know I wanted to stay there, but my father made me leave."

"It's okay. I didn't want you to see me like that anyway," he answered honestly. We sat in silence for a moment as my stomach flipped, and I felt like a kid talking to my crush, not knowing what to say. It was ridiculous since we'd already slept together. "Come spend the day with me."

"Is than an order?" I teased, biting my nail, nervous about how he would respond.

"It's a request, bella. I want to see you."

I smiled wide, biting my bottom lip. Something had changed the night before when I thought his life was in danger and realized the truth about my feelings. Now, talking to him felt both awkward and exhilarating. I hoped he was starting to feel the same way.

"What time do you want me to meet you and where?"

"Be ready in thirty. I'm coming to pick you up."

When we hung up, I rushed to my room to change my clothes. I had already taken my shower and freshened up earlier. One benefit to not sleeping, I guess. We hadn't talked about where we were going, so I decided to dress comfortably. I picked out a pair of matching black lace bra and panties, figuring it wouldn't hurt to be ready for anything. When it came to Marc, we always seemed to end up naked, or partially naked, and I wasn't going to say no. At least, not today. After pulling on my favorite pair of distressed jeans that were so soft they felt like sweats, I paired them with a black tank top under a thin, yellow cardigan. I left my hair long and wavy and only added a little mascara and neutral-colored gloss. I finished the look with a couple of longer necklaces I loved to layer and my gold hooped earrings right as Marcello texted to let me know he had arrived.

I left a note on the fridge for Harper, telling her not to wait up and hurried down to Marc. I was so excited to see him. My breath caught when I exited my building and saw him leaning against the SUV with his ankles crossed and arms folded in front of him. His hair was styled perfectly, and his dark aviator shades made him look hot as hell. He seemed to have the same idea of wearing jeans with a tight, plain black shirt that showed off his muscular arms. Not wanting to overthink about things, I let my emotions lead me as I ran up to him and threw my arms around his neck in a big hug. His arms wrapped around me tightly, not moving to pull away. After a beat, I leaned back and kissed him sweetly on the lips.

"I'm glad to see that you're up and moving," I whispered.

"I'm happy to see you so happy, bella," he smiled and gave me a quick peck on the lips. "Let's get some lunch."

I backed away enough for him to stand straight and open the back door for me to slide in. I was surprised to see Shane and Dante in the front seats. *How did I not see them when I came out?* Maybe because my focus was on the hot Italian that would soon be my husband.

"How's it going, Mila?" Shane asked as he looked at me through the rearview mirror from the driver's seat.

"Better," I admitted.

Marc slid in beside me, and Shane edged us out into traffic.

"Where would you like to eat?" he asked as he threaded his fingers between mine and rested our joined hands in his lap.

"Anywhere that has good food and privacy. I have questions."

"I would be worried if you didn't," he admitted and offered me a gentle smile. "Take us to Craft on Constellation Boulevard," he told Shane.

I leaned close to Marcello so that his guys in the front couldn't hear. "Is there a reason we won't be able to have alone time?"

"Who said we wouldn't?" he asked with a mischievous grin and a twinkle in his eye that made my stomach dip in anticipation.

"Will they at least give us space?"

"We will have our privacy. After last night, I can't exactly waltz around on my own. Everyone's too nervous."

"Just as you should be, jackass," Dante chimed in from the front passenger seat. "You thinking that you're untouchable is what got you into that mess in the first place."

"Fuck off, Dante," Marc responded, but he was smiling. It worried me that he wasn't taking the situation seriously.

Shane and Dante followed us into the restaurant, and we were seated out on the terrace at Marc's request. He also paid the hostess extra to keep the tables around us empty. Shane and Dante sat at the opposite end of the terrace but made sure they had a clear visual of our table.

We both ordered Mahi Mahi with potatoes and an avocado salad with a couple different cocktails. When Marc took off his sunglasses, the sunlight highlighted his injuries. There was a large bruise on the left side of his face as well as a black eye starting to form on the right.

"Jesus, does that hurt?" I asked as I started to reach across the table to touch his face but decided against it and returned my hand to my lap.

"It's nothing I can't handle."

"Please explain to me what happened. Everyone was so worried."

I watched as he studied me before turning away to stare into the distance. I couldn't tell if he would open up, but I hoped he would. I watched as he took a big drink of his cocktail before returning his attention back to me. I realized that in moment I was holding my breath and tried to let it out without bringing attention to that fact.

"It was stupid, to be honest. Shane had offered to follow me as I took out my bike for a ride. I needed to clear my head, and there is a spot out in the hills that I love to visit when I need the quiet. Shane even warned me people may try to strike against us with news of our wedding spreading, but like an arrogant ass, I told him there was nothing to worry about."

"Then what happened? It looked like you were mauled by an animal," I said quietly.

"A van pulled out in front of me, so I had to bail."

My eyes grew wide at the realization of how bad his injuries could be. I remained quiet for him to continue, but my worry for him started to come back to the surface.

"They tied me up and took me to a rundown motel. That's when I realized who had taken me and that I wasn't really in too much danger."

"Not in too much danger? You could have been killed, Marc," I hissed across the table. I hated that he acted as though it was all no big deal at all.

"The guys who grabbed me were small fish. Bottom feeders, really. My father had already talked about pushing them out. With them taking me last night, it's now a done deal, which I'm happy about. They were a pain in my ass and brought too much trouble."

Our server brought out our plates and asked if we needed anything. When she left, I urged Marc to keep going. I wanted to know everything, especially while he was in the mood to share.

"Why did they grab you?"

"It was over something stupid," he shrugged as he took a bite of his food.

"Marc," I urged. He took a deep breath as he chewed another bite. I could tell he didn't want to tell me, which made me nervous.

"One of the guys was the brother of a girl I used to date on and off. She had diluted ideas of what our relationship was, and they thought they could somehow blackmail me into marrying her instead. They knew my father was pushing them out, and them grabbing me was their last-ditch effort to stay in the game."

I took in what he said as I took a bite of my fish. I could feel his eyes on me. "I thought you don't date," was all I said. I instantly regretted it the moment it left my lips, knowing I sounded like a jealous girlfriend. I had heard here and there about all of the DeLuca boys being players, especially "the one that dated the oldest Fedorov daughter." Marc's smile grew across his face as he watched me. "What?"

"You're jealous," he said.

He's liking this. I tried to deny his statement with no success. We both knew exactly how I sounded, and if I were being honest, I did hate that there were more than just Anya from his past who meant more to him than a quick lay. *How could I be more upset about him dating than him being a player?*

"Do we need to worry about them striking again since they didn't get what they wanted?" I asked, desperate to change the subject.

"The truth is, there will always be the threat of someone striking against us. Either as a couple or just because of who our families are. But you have to know I would never let anything happen to you. Your safety will always be a priority for me." He reached over the table with his palm up for me to take his hand. I slid my small hand into his big one, and he squeezed. "I know I have been an ass, Mila. But I'm hoping this can be my second chance. I want to show you that I can be a good partner."

"I appreciate you wanting to try. I hope that means you will always be honest with me, no matter how bad things get."

He looked at me quizzically with his head cocked

slightly. "Does this mean you are finally accepting our marriage and wanting to make it work?"

Shit, shit, shit. Is that what I was saying? I felt so torn. A part of me wanted to fully commit and see where this life could go. To see where this love could go. But there was still another part of me that wanted to run. I didn't want to be controlled. I wanted a chance to live a life I love, and I wasn't sure I could have that if I stayed in LA. I decided to keep him positive until I could answer him fully. I couldn't cause suspicion if I decided to still leave.

"If you can promise to give me freedom and not control every aspect of my life, yes."

"Bella, there are some things you will want me to take control of." His voice was lower and laced with promise. I knew his statement had a double meaning, but I was instantly turned on by the sexual tone resting between the lines.

We continued our lunch with light banter and ideas of where to go for our honeymoon. It was surreal to talk to him as if we had been together for years. It felt so natural. I hated that the worry and doubt remained in the back of my mind.

After our lunch, Shane dropped us off at a bike dealership. There were a handful of beautiful motorcycles outside as well as on the floor inside the building.

"Are they already done fixing your bike?" I asked, confused, as Marcello led me inside the building.

"I'm buying a new one, and you're going to pick it out."

"There you go telling me what to do," I teased. "I know nothing about bikes, Marc. I would be the worst person to make this choice."

"Lucky for you, I've had my eye on three, so you only need to pick from them. Let me show you."

He grabbed my hand and took me to an office at the end of the building to meet a salesman that knew Marc by his first name. The man led us to the back, through the mechanic's shop, and then out to the back of the building where three beautiful bikes sat. Then the salesman left us alone to make our decision.

Marc pointed to a silver bike at the end that looked like it was from the future. "This is the Kawasaki H2R," he explained, then moved on to the other two. "This is a Ducati, much like the one I just totaled. And this last one is the Triumph Rocket 3."

"These are all so beautiful," I gushed, looking at the bikes, unsure how to choose. "I really can't pick. They are all great."

"Come on, bella. Which one would you like to ride with me?"

I looked at him with round eyes. I had never been on a bike before. Hearing of his recent accident, I wasn't sure I wanted to. Although, there was something sexy about the idea of riding on the back of a bike, holding on to Marc's rock-hard chest.

"The Triumph then. It's sleek, beautiful, and looks the most comfortable for me to ride with you."

"You got it."

He led me back to the main showroom, and we sat down with the salesman. Once all the necessary paperwork was filled out, Marc shook hands with the guy and was given the keys. We stopped and grabbed two matching helmets and a pair of gloves for him. After a quick call to Shane, he led us back to where the bikes were and handed me a helmet.

"Hop on. I want to show you one of my favorite places."

CHAPTER
NINE
MARCELLO

MILA MADE a great choice to go with the Triumph. I loved feeling her hands on me as we glided through the hills. I was a little anxious taking the same route as the other day, but the odds of me getting stopped again were slim. Plus, Shane and Dante were trailing us. I told them to leave enough space so that we could be alone, but they refused to let me out of their sight.

We came to a clearing at the top of a hill off of Mulholland Drive that overlooked the bustling city below. The sun was high and the breeze perfect. I parked the bike to the side, where it was slightly hidden behind a hill for one side of the traffic, but Shane could still see from where he was parked. I needed some privacy with my girl. I needed to make up for leaving her hanging in my suite. I felt like shit for doing it. She didn't deserve it. She and I were going to be equals, and I wanted her to know that. Sure, I still wanted control in the bedroom, but I would never leave her wanting again if I could help it.

I pulled off my helmet and rested it on a handlebar

before getting off the bike. Then I turned to help Mila with her helmet and set it on the other handle. She started getting off the bike, but I stopped her. She looked like a goddess sitting on the sleek black metal with the breeze flowing through her hair.

"You're a vision, bella," I said huskily.

I was so taken by her beauty that it was as though I couldn't get my words out. She just smiled at me, biting her bottom lip, which made my cock twitch with need. I stepped closer and slid my hand into her silky, soft hair, pulling her to me for a kiss. Her hands rested on my chest, sending a magnetic current through my body, her vanilla scent whirling around us.

The kiss deepened quickly. My hands roamed all over her body as hers pulled me as close as I could get without knocking the bike over. I slid her cardigan off her shoulders and kissed her beautiful, tanned skin. I peeked behind us to make sure the guys couldn't see us, and they couldn't. Knowing we had our privacy, I pulled Mila's tank top straps down with the front so that it tucked under her breasts. Then I grabbed each mound, kissing her through the black lace.

"I've been dreaming about these tits," I moaned, kissing my way back up to her lips as she buried her hands in my hair.

I pulled a nipple free from her bra, twisting it between my fingertips, making her moan into my mouth. Her movements became frantic, trying to get my clothes off as well as her bra. She left her tank around her middle, not caring to take the time to strip completely. I unbuttoned her jeans, and she lifted her ass for me to pull them off of her. I stepped back for a moment to admire her sitting in just her pushed down tank and black lace panties, perched on top of a beautiful piece of machinery, the sunlight as her spotlight. She was picture perfect.

"Are you done gawking?" she teased.

"Never," I replied in awe.

She motioned for me to come back to her with her finger, and I obliged. I didn't want to wait any longer. I needed to feel her, and she seemed to have the same need. I grabbed her cardigan and laid it out on the grass next to the bike. I helped her off the bike and down onto the ground. We shared a deep, passionate kiss as she helped to remove my jeans and boxers. I hovered over her as I reached between us and slid two fingers inside her already wet and ready pussy.

"Mmm," she moaned as I pumped my fingers inside of her, making her come quickly as she squeezed her fingers into my arm.

Before she could come down from her orgasm, I quickly replaced my fingers with my cock that was hard as stone and buried myself as deeply as I could, taking a moment to feel her walls convulse around me. She lifted her legs and wrapped them around me for a better angle as I started moving in and out.

"Faster," she breathed.

She didn't need to say it twice. We moved together in a rhythm that was going to send us both over the fucking edge in a matter of minutes. I could feel myself tighten as I became close to releasing my load. I thrust deep and held it for a moment, trying to regain control so that I could get her to cum one last time.

"Fuck me, Marc. I'm so close," she begged as she moved her hips, anxious for her release.

I rammed into her fast and hard, grunting with the buildup. She felt so fucking good, but we both needed it to be quick and intense to release the tension from the past two days. With one final thrust, we both hollered out as we came together. I didn't care if the fellas heard us. I rested my head next to hers as our bodies stopped shaking and our breathing regulated. Without saying a word, I kissed the tip of her nose and gently pulled out of her.

Once we were dressed, we sat on the hill and watched the sky and the view below. We didn't need to say anything. Just sitting there in peace with each other's presence was enough. My heart swelled for the woman sitting next to me, and it was hitting me like a freight train. I was falling for Mila, and I didn't want to fight it. I wanted to be with her. I wanted to build a life with her. Give her the world. I just prayed I would measure up to be the man she deserved and that she would give me the chance to prove myself to her.

I let the hot water wash over me as steam filled the shower. I could still feel Mila's body. I could still smell her. I wanted to bring her back to my place after our ride out to the hills, but I had better plans. Instead, I took her home and told her to rest. Little did she know I was planning a getaway for us to get out of LA and away from the chaos. I needed time with my bella to really tell her how I felt and to make sure we wanted the same things. The more time I spent with her, the more her happiness mattered to me more than anything else. But I was also realizing I wouldn't want to be with anyone else. She had begun knocking down all the walls I had built to keep myself from getting close to people. She made me *want* to open up to her. She was the first person to make me feel safe, which was a fucking odd feeling.

I prided myself on being the provider and protector, the embodiment of what it meant to be a man. But I somehow knew I could be vulnerable with Mila and that she would protect me just as fiercely. She was the daughter of the Don, after all. I would be disappointed if she was weak and needed to be taken care of. It was different to provide for a strong woman who didn't need you versus someone who couldn't survive without you. She had a fire to her that she would never let anyone put out, no matter what. That same fire made me nervous and worried that she might not want the life I could offer her. I couldn't get away from the mafia life. It was in my DNA. And some would argue the same about her if it weren't for the fact that she'd rebelled every step of the way. She'd made a point to be as far away from the life as possible. Would she be willing to stay for us to be together? Would she willingly walk down the aisle? Or would she resent me for life once we say "I do"?

I finished my shower, more eager to get away with Mila to solidify our goals, to solidify our relationship and discuss what we both wanted and expected moving forward. I changed into some comfortable traveling clothes and packed a bag for the weekend. I sent a text to Mila, telling her to pack for a weekend away and that she would be picked up shortly. I then went over my plans with Shane and told him he needed to make himself scarce.

"You're not going alone, Marcello."

"I know that, Shane. Once we touch down in Lake Tahoe, you can follow us at a distance, but once we are near the cabin, you need to stay somewhere else. We won't leave, and I will call you if anything happens."

"This is risky, man," Shane said with doubt, shaking

his head. "Especially when you won't let anyone else come. What if someone else tries to pull a Bruno?"

"Bruno got lucky and caught me off guard. That won't happen again. Besides, this is a last-minute trip. I only just now called the pilot to set the flight plan with the jet. He assured me no one had plans to use it until our honeymoon. No one will know we left, and no one will find us, unless you open your big mouth. I need this to happen, Shane."

"Fine," he huffed. "Do you need me to go pick up your bride?" I smiled at his question. Shane calling Mila my bride hit me differently. "You look like a love-struck idiot."

"Maybe I am," I countered. "Please, go pack your bag and then grab Mila. Meet me at the hanger within the hour."

Shane left to do as I'd asked, and I made a few stops before heading to the hanger. I wasn't sure when was the last time someone went to the cabin, so I grabbed some provisions in case the cabinets and fridge were bare. Though, I didn't plan to spend much time outside of the bedroom or outside of Mila.

I smiled so wide when Shane pulled up with Mila that my face felt as if it would break in half. She looked divine in white leggings and black boots that stopped just below her knee. She wore an oversized black, cable-knit sweater with the red ski jacket slung over her arm that I had Shane stop and buy for her.

"Where are you taking me, DeLuca?" Her smile lit me up.

"You'll have to wait and see," I answered before lowering to kiss her lightly on the lips.

The three of us piled into the cabin of my family jet. It was a short trip, and I was eager to get there. I put the grocery bags in the upper cabinets with our overnight bags.

"Groceries? Should I be worried?" Mila teased as we sat on a bench seat along the side of the cabin.

"It's beautiful. You'll love it," I assured her.

Mila snuggled into my side after we buckled our seatbelts. Shane stayed at the back of the cabin in a seat next to a window.

"How are we lucky enough to only have one shadow?" Mila whispered.

"We don't need any more than that. Please, don't worry. We'll be safe. I promise."

Within ninety minutes, we touched down in Lake Tahoe, where two tinted SUVs were waiting. Shane helped us load everything into our vehicle before disappearing into his. I took my place behind the wheel, grabbing Mila's hand in mine before we set off for our final destination. We talked about meaningless things and sang some songs. But I mostly listened to Mila sing. It was amazing to see her drop her guard and really open up. She was so free.

She gushed about the scenery as we neared the family cabin. Shane turned off a mile back, honoring his promise to remain scarce.

"This is amazing! We are only a few hours from LA and there is snow everywhere," she admired as we pulled up.

"Have you never left LA?"

"Only when I lived in Russia before graduating."

She hopped out of the car and instantly started shaking and wrapping her arms around herself. "Jesus, it's cold!"

"That's why you have a ski jacket," I teased. "Go inside while I grab the bags. There should be a key in the left light fixture by the door."

I chuckled as I watched her jog to the porch, struggling to get her jacket on quick enough. I slung our bags over my shoulder and grabbed the three grocery bags with our food and drinks. When I walked in the door, Mila was standing in the center of the room, looking around in awe.

"This is beautiful!"

"It's one of our safe houses, but it doesn't get used much, which is sad because it's stunning up here," I answered as I set the groceries on the counter in the small kitchen.

Then I moved to drop our bags on the king-sized bed in the only bedroom of the cabin. It was mostly open space, with a large stone fireplace as the main attraction. There was a vaulted ceiling that housed a loft area, where we kept two twin beds and a dresser for when there was a group of us staying. There were various decorations to add to the log cabin aesthetic, including a large bookcase with books and games strewn about the shelves.

"I hate to complain, but it's freezing in here," Mila laughed.

"There should be wood around the back. I'll be right back."

I grabbed a basket by the fireplace and filled it with wood. I started a fire as quickly as I could before going back for more wood and leaving it on the hearth for later. Mila stood in front of the flames with her hands held out to soak in the warmth. I walked up to her and pulled her to me, hoping I would be able to help warm her up.

"So, what was your plan bringing me up here?" she asked as she looked up at me with a ridiculous grin, her emerald eyes bright.

"Would you be disappointed if I said I didn't have

plans outside of that bedroom?" I motioned to the room behind us.

"Not one bit," she giggled before rising on her tiptoes for a quick kiss. "How long are we staying?"

"Just the night. We have to get back to finalize everything for the wedding." I watched as the light in her eyes dimmed slightly, though she tried to hide it. "But we can come here whenever you want afterwards. The lake is breathtaking, and there are amazing trails to hike."

"Sounds perfect." She smiled up at me, then rested her head on my chest as we watched the flames.

It didn't take long for the cabin to warm up and we could take off our jackets. We put the groceries away and poured a glass of wine before cuddling up on the couch.

"I did have another reason for this trip," I said after a long moment of silence. My heart started to speed up, worried that our trip wouldn't go as planned. Worried that she would run the moment I opened up to her.

"Oh?" she asked over her glass before taking a sip.

"Yeah." I cleared my throat to cover my nerves. "I wanted to talk about us. About our future."

She stopped her glass mid-tilt and stared at me over the rim. She slowly took a long swig of her wine before placing her glass on the coffee table in front of us. "What about it?"

"Mila, I know we didn't start out in the best way. The strain of us being together just for the sake of keeping our families' legacies alive messed things up for us right from the beginning. I have to admit that I wasn't keen on the idea and didn't plan on us actually having a real relationship."

"Wait, what do you mean you didn't plan on us having a real relationship? We're meant to be married."

"I know. And many men in both of our families got away with the image of a stable homelife and wife while having someone on the side whom they really wanted to be with."

"A mistress!?" her voice hitched high, and her eyes were wide with fire. She was ready for an argument, letting me know I had already managed to fuck up the conversation. *Fuck.*

CHAPTER
TEN
MARCELLO

"PLEASE, let me explain before you get fired up," I pleaded as I sat straighter in my seat and set my glass down. Our conversation had taken a turn in the wrong direction, and I needed to get it back on track. I turned so that I was facing her, and she could see my eyes as I spoke. "This was all my thought process before meeting you and getting to know you. I know it's a shit way to think, believe me. But the more time we spent together, the more my mindset changed. *I* changed."

"How so?"

"Bella," I started but stopped to think about how I wanted to phrase the next part. I didn't want to fuck it up. I grabbed her hands in mine before continuing. "I don't know when it happened. Perhaps when you played my mother's cello, but somewhere in the last week and a half, something inside me shifted completely. I want to see you every day. I go to sleep thinking about you, I dream about you, and then I wake up thinking about you and figuring out ways to see you. I know it sounds insane. We barely know each other. But you feel like home to me, Mila. As though we have lived many lives together and finally found one another in this one. Marrying you no longer feels like an arranged duty I am being forced to carry out. I look forward to seeing you walk toward me in a white dress, knowing that you are tying your life to mine. But I need to know you feel the same. I need to know that you want this the same as I do."

My heart was pounding in my chest, and I could hear it in my ears. I knew my palms were sweating, but I thought that if I let her hands go, she would drift away. I had never opened up that way to anyone and feared she would make me regret it. That she didn't feel the same and didn't want to marry me. She sat there looking at our joined hands in silence, making me panic even more. But when she lifted her face to mine, she had tears running down her face.

"I feel like I'm in an impossible position, Marc. I can't deny that there is something between us. You've managed to work your way into my heart even when I wanted to hate you. I've even caught myself imagining what life would be like for us. But then I remember who we are, and I am reminded that I am being forced into a life I despise and am being refused the life I've dreamt of."

My heart broke as she spoke. I knew she wasn't happy about the arrangement, but I never realized just how much I hated that I was connected to the source of her anguish.

"How can I make this easier for you, bella?"

"I don't know. Let me have my business, for starters."

"I can't do that, Mila. I've told you that." I released her hands and sat forward, moving to the edge of the couch. I downed the rest of my wine and rested my elbows on my knees. I didn't want to keep telling her no, but I refused to let her work with that piece of shit, George Martin.

"You've never told me why, Marc. You've been the only one in the way of opening my own record label, besides my father. Why are you so adamant about keeping it from happening? How would it hurt you or your business?"

I rose from the couch and started pacing. I didn't want to have this conversation. Not when I wanted this time to be for us to become closer. Stronger.

"It doesn't hurt me one bit, Mila."

"Then why?" she yelled. She was now on her feet and standing in front of me, forcing us to speak face to face. "Why are you determined to help ruin my life?"

I stared at her dumbfounded. She thought I was trying to ruin her life. Why wouldn't she? Not only was she being forced to marry me, but she was also being denied the one thing she wanted, and I was involved in both scenarios.

"Then let's make a deal. You ditch Martin, and I will approve your label," I offered.

"No. He's been there for me the last two years, teaching me as much as possible about the music industry. Not to mention the connections he has and that he's the one backing the cost to get us started."

"I'll give you the money then."

"Absolutely not."

"Why? How would me paying for it be any different than you letting that piece of shit pay?"

"Why do you hate him so much?"

"Answer the question, Mila."

"Because he would be a partner. He would be in it with me, making sure it's successful. It's not just about the money. Plus, you helping me would be the same as my father helping me, and I refuse to do that. There was an understanding that I would pay George back the money for getting my business off the ground. He understands my need to do this on my own. I don't want my business tied to the mafia or its dirty money."

"Careful, bella." I gritted my teeth to keep my temper in check.

I knew there were still some parts of our businesses that dealt with not so legal means of obtaining money, but I had been working to change all of that. I had no control over how things were done in the past.

Mila stepped up to me and looked me straight in the eyes. "Or what?"

With a growl, I dug my hand into her hair and around to the nape of her neck, grabbed a fistful of her hair, and pulled her head back so that I had her in place but didn't hurt her. She was scowling up at me, but her cheeks reddened like they did when she was turned on. My temper became laced with desire the moment I looked at her lips. I crushed my mouth to hers, stealing a not so sweet kiss. She surprised me by biting my bottom lip.

"Fuck, Mila," I hissed, bringing my fingers to my lip where she drew blood.

I looked at her, and she was laughing. Her emerald eyes were a dark green, and her pupils were huge. My dick hardened excitedly against the confines of my pants at the anticipation of some rough foreplay. Not many could feed my needs in this way. Mila stood out from any other woman in every respect thus far. Why wouldn't she stand out with this too?

Before I could make another move, she surprised me by hooking her leg around the back of mine. She pushed me backward, making me fall, and she came with me as I grabbed her arms on my way down. I hit the ground hard, and she fell on top of me. My body still ached from skidding across the pavement when I was taken, but I didn't want her to know that.

She buried her hands in my hair and pulled it back so that my throat was exposed. She nipped and nibbled at my flesh, making me develop goosebumps all over my body. I was so turned on while also confused with the sudden change of power. I liked it. I slid my hand to her ass, but she quickly reached back and slapped my hand away. I did it again with my other hand, but this time, she bit my earlobe, making me yelp. Learning the new rules as we went, I pressed my hands to the cold hardwood floor to keep from touching her. I wanted to see how far she would take things.

She moved down my body, lifting the hem of my shirt to kiss my abs. I tried to keep my breathing in check, but she had me so worked up.

"Take it off," she demanded, pushing the hem of my shirt to my chest.

I obeyed this goddess and quickly removed my shirt as she unbuckled my pants and started pulling them down my legs, along with my boxer briefs. When I tried to help, she bit my thigh.

"Fuck, Mila. You're in tender territory there," I warned.

I didn't want to scare her, but I still had wounds on my body from my bike accident, and my legs and hip seemed to have taken the brunt of it. She slowed her movements slightly as she pushed my pants to my ankles but didn't take them off. She sat on her knees and looked at the scratches and cuts along my thighs and shins.

I watched as she barely touched the wounds with the tips of her fingers. She took my breath away when she bent down and gently kissed every one of them. A lump formed in my throat at the sudden shift of energy and her display of love and care. My breathing became harder as I tried to fight the tears I felt threatening to fall from the corners of my eyes. She gently moved my legs apart and settled herself between them. She kissed my thighs, making my hard cock bounce involuntarily. She gently wrapped her small hand around the shaft and looked up at me as she licked the pre-cum from the tip cock. A tear fell down the side of my face, and I didn't try to stop it.

Her eyebrows bunched with concern, but she continued taking me into her mouth, never shifting her eyes off mine. She slid her legs flat so that she was laying on her stomach between my legs, sliding her mouth up and down my shaft. One of her hands moved to massage my abs and my sides as she sucked me off, bringing a whole new level of intimacy. It didn't take long for me to feel my balls tighten with the warning that I was going to come.

"You gotta stop, bella. I'm too close," I warned.

She looked back up at me with a twinkle in her eye. She grasped my shaft tightly as she slid her mouth up and down faster, making sure to lick the tip every few passes. She was driving me crazy, but I tried to hold on as long as I could.

"Almost there, Mila," I moaned, letting my head fall back with my eyes closed.

Suddenly, with a pop, she let my cock fall out of her mouth and slap onto my belly. I instantly sat up on my elbows to see what the fuck she was doing. I was two seconds from unloading in that beautiful mouth. But she lay between my legs with her head in her hands, her feet kicking in the air, with an expression as sweet as could be.

"What the fuck, Mila?" I bit out.

"Not such a great feeling, is it?"

Fuck. I knew she was pissed about the way I left her in my suite back home. I felt terrible for it but never dreamed she would want payback. "Stop playing games."

"You're the one who started it."

"I'm sorry, okay? I've felt like shit about doing that to you. I was trying to prove a point that obviously doesn't need to be made." She tilted her head and just looked at me with a grin while my body was on fire. I needed a release so bad, and I was desperate for her to be the one to do it. "Please, Mila. I'm sorry," I begged. Never in a million years would have I ever thought that I would be begging a woman to finish blowing me, nor would I ever admit it, but here we were.

"Well, lucky for you, I'm not a raging douche," she said chipperly.

She then grasped my still hard cock and vigorously sucked and licked until I was ready to explode.

"I'm going to cum," I warned so that she could make the decision to let it go or take it in her mouth. Surprisingly, she sucked me through it, taking it all in one gulp. She sat up on her knees, licking her lips with the most adorable smile.

"Fuck, bella".

I sat up and pulled her into my lap so that she was straddling me. I gently caressed her cheek with my thumb before kissing her. I felt another tear escape as I was overwhelmed with new depths of emotions I had only heard about. She had just taken me for a roller coaster ride of emotions, and I loved every minute of it. She reached up, wiped the tears from my skin, and kissed the tip of my nose.

"I'm falling for you, Mila Fedorov," I admitted in the moment of vulnerability.

This time, she was the one letting tears fall. I kissed her cheeks, licking her tears away in the process.

"I'm falling for you, too, Marcello DeLuca, and it terrifies me."

CHAPTER
ELEVEN

MILA

THE SUN WARMED my face as it streamed in through the small window in the bedroom of the cabin. I was laying on my side with Marc's arms wrapped tightly around me from behind. I tried not to move so that I wouldn't wake him as I watched the sky through the window and listened to the birds singing outside.

We hadn't make any headway on the music business front, but we had made progress, nonetheless. I was overwhelmed with emotions as I saw tears falling from his eyes when I kissed the scratches from his accident on the night he was taken. I wondered if he had never been shown any level of love. I could feel him open up, especially when he was fine with turning control over to me, sexually. I wanted so badly to hear the things he was saying to me, but it was gutting me all the same. I just wasn't sure, yet, if I would be able to walk away from Marc when it came down to the wire.

After last night, I knew that I was in love with Marcello, but I wasn't convinced I still wouldn't run. I refused to give up on my dream, and I refused to do it with any help from mafia money. Until he gave me a straight answer about George, I wouldn't walk away from that partnership. Even though on paper he was listed as just a silent investor, he had helped me too much for me to not continue treating him as a partner. George was the only one that seemed to believe in me and wanted to do what he could to help make it happen for me.

I felt Marc start to stir behind me, then I felt him slide his erection under my ass cheeks and between my thighs. I instinctively arched my back and opened my legs, feeling the head of his cock lightly kissing my sensitive pussy lips at the bottom of my opening. I smiled, knowing that with one slight adjustment, he could slide right in.

"Good morning, my bella," he whispered in my ear, sending chills down my spine in the most inviting way. "How about we start this morning off right with a morning ride?"

I smiled and pushed my ass into him as he continued to slide himself between my thighs. I bit my bottom lip as he reached a hand around to the front of me, parting my lips to expose my swollen bean. He started to rub me in a gentle circle, making me wet with the sensation.

I was still so sensitive from our lovemaking the night before. After we had our disagreement on the living room floor, he carried me to the bed, where we worshipped one another multiple times. I could say I was thoroughly fucked. I wasn't sure I could take anymore without giving myself some time to recoup.

With a groan, I stopped his hand. "For as much as I want to continue our sexcapades, I really need to rest. And eat."

He kissed my bare shoulder, pulling me tighter to

him in a hug. "Are you sure?" he asked as he thrust against me one last time.

"Unfortunately," I said with a sigh.

"How about you hop in the shower while I make us some breakfast?"

Marc got up from the bed and stepped into a fresh pair of boxers before heading out into the kitchen. I smiled as I stretched in the bed. I knew we still had to talk about some things, but I felt a lot better about the potential of our relationship, if I could just make a final decision about leaving.

Once I showered and dressed in warm clothes, I met Marcello in the kitchen, where he had pancakes and fruit waiting for me along with freshly-brewed coffee.

"OMG, this looks great. I didn't know you could cook."

"This is your first time staying the night with me. You hadn't had that luxury yet," he smiled as he popped a strawberry into his mouth. He was adorable sitting half naked with me at the breakfast table, his hair mussed and a slight stubble on his face.

"Are you up for a short hike today?"

"I would love that," I gushed. "I've been dying to see the sights since we drove up here."

"Good. After we eat, I'll get ready and take you to see the water. It's incredible — the lake looks like a reflection of the blue sky, mostly and surrounded by the beautiful Sierra Nevada Mountains. Then, tonight, when we get back home, I want to take you to dinner. Does that sound okay?"

"What are you planning, DeLuca?" I teased.

He gave me a crooked grin that made me feel giddy. "You'll have to wait and see."

After breakfast, we bundled up, and I followed

Marc along a path that must had been created years ago. The scenery was so serene and calming, I couldn't wait to come out in the summer. *You're making plans, Mila. Is this proof of my decision?*

As we came to a clearing, a lake with the most beautiful blue water expanded before us. There were snow-capped peaks in the distance, with an assortment of gigantic pine trees. The sun bounced off the water, giving it a magical look.

"This is surreal," I breathed as I took it all in.

"Favolosa."

When I turned to look at him, I realized he was looking at me when he answered. My heart swelled at the love I could see looking back at me. My heart feathered in my chest, making me feel out of body. I couldn't believe I was in the most beautiful place with Marcello DeLuca, the most gorgeous man I had ever seen, and he was all mine, and I was his.

He showed me a few more of his favorite spots along the same path before we had to head back and get ready to leave. We met Shane at the hanger, where he had already instructed the pilot to prepare for lift-off. When we were back in Los Angelas, Marc dropped me off at my apartment long enough for me to get ready for dinner. I was a ball of nerves when he instructed me to dress in a gown.

Harper had an amazing gold dress with tactful sequins that I had been dying for a chance to borrow. She helped me curl and wind my hair up into an elegant up-do before she went out with Jacob. She made sure to remind me of our plans to leave in a couple of days. My acquaintance had dropped off the envelope with our new documents while I was away. I didn't have the heart to tell Harper I was having second thoughts — she was so excited about New

York. So I decided I wouldn't bring it up unless I made a concrete decision to stay.

Marcello arrived just after eight to pick me up for dinner. This time, he had Shane and his younger brother, Dominic, in tow.

"Damn, Mila," Dominic expressed as he opened the car door for me. "You look fine as hell!"

"Watch it," Marc warned from inside the SUV.

Dominic raised his hands in surrender but then winked at me before closing the door. I couldn't help but laugh.

"Don't encourage him," Marc chided. "You do look stunning, though."

"You look pretty good yourself," I answered as I took in the sight of him.

His hair was styled into place, and his stubble gone. He wore a midnight blue suit that I could tell had been perfectly tailored to him. His white dress shirt underneath was left open at the top, revealing Marcello's tanned skin, accented with an elegant, gold chain. The scent of his cologne was mixed with cinnamon this time, making me wonder if he had used a special soap just for our date. *How precious.* I loved the thought of him fretting over how he smelt only for dinner with me.

When we pulled up to the restaurant, I was pleased to see Shane and Marc's brother not only staying in the car but pulling away.

"Wow, they're giving us space without you having to bribe them," I teased as we walked inside, making him smile.

The restaurant was stunning and another place I had yet to visit. The aesthetic was warm and romantic, with dim lighting and candles lit all throughout the building. Most tables were occupied by couples, other than a few exceptions with no more than four at a table.

The hostess led us all the way to the back of the restaurant to a table that was separate from the rest and next to a beautiful fireplace. There was already Champagne chilling in a bucket at our table with a beautiful, short bouquet of flowers in the center and two tall candles alight. My heart started racing at what was on display and what it could mean. Marc pulled out my chair for me before sitting on the other side of the table.

"This is nice, Marc," I offered as he poured us a glass of bubbly. He handed me one and held his between us to indicate he was going to make a toast, so I followed suit.

"Here's to an amazing trip to Lake Tahoe and many more to come."

My heart raced a little faster, and I could feel my cheeks flush. I smiled at him like an idiot and clinked my glass to his before taking a huge drink. *Did I decide on this? Am I staying?*

"What would you like to eat?" Marc asked as he handed me a small menu.

I looked it over a few times. But I couldn't focus on reading the items when my mind was racing. I couldn't decide on whether I had landed on a final answer while fighting the excitement of sitting in such a romantic restaurant with Marcello. Trying to focus on the items listed in front of me, I decided on sirloin and broccoli, which he ordered as well.

"Listen, I know I avoided giving you a solid answer about George Martin," Marc started, putting me on alert. I didn't want to fight. "So, I owe you one, and I hope you will seriously consider walking away from him when I'm done."

"I'm listening," I answered.

"Not only did we find out he was using one of our business connections to smuggle in drugs, but he was also being accused of multiple assaults from various women."

"You're joking," I scoffed.

"Unfortunately, no."

"Then how is he not in prison?"

"We couldn't get enough evidence to stick. No matter how many women came forward, he would still manage to walk away with just a slap on the wrist. When I found out he was trying for a license in the music industry, it made me sick to think of the women he would have access to, so I blocked it at every turn. I don't want you working with him, bella. I know he may not seem like a threat to you, but I promise you, he's bad news. I need you safe. If you don't want to take money from me, then at least let me help you get a loan to get you started. You don't need him."

I took a moment to let what he had said sink in. There were a few times where George weirded me out, but did I believe he was a serial troublemaker? I looked at Marc and saw the seriousness in his eyes. *Why would he lie to me?*

"I'll break ties with George, but what makes you think it won't trigger him to come after me?"

"He won't try to come near you. We'll make sure of it."

I studied Marcello a moment more, deciding I would trust him about George. "Fine, but we will talk more about the loan idea later. I don't want to ruin this beautiful dinner."

"I have one more thing to get off my chest. Then we can soak up every second of the evening."

My heart pounded and my hair stood on end as he got out of his seat and knelt in front of me.

"Mila, I may have started out as a royal pain in the ass, but you've softened my stone heart. You've changed me for the better. I want to know what our future holds, but I don't want to see it without you." He pulled out a black velvet box and opened it to show a blinding diamond twice the size of my finger. "Will you marry me, bella?"

Tears filled my eyes as I looked at the man I loved who was on one knee, asking me to be his forever partner. At that moment, I decided to stay. I decided I wanted a life with Marcello and that it was too special to walk away from.

"Yes," I whispered as tears fell down my cheeks.

Marcello stood and pulled me to him with a deep kiss. When we pulled away, he slid the ring onto my finger, kissing the skin once it was in place.

"I love you, Mila."

TWELVE
MILA

SITTING AT MY KITCHEN TABLE, I watched the sun hit my engagement ring as I stirred my coffee. I was lost on how I could go from being determined to get out of dodge to deciding to stay within twenty-four hours. To be fair, it was many little things building up to Marc proposing to me, but the trip to Lake Tahoe had sealed it for me somehow. But now that I was away from Marcello and back in my own head, I wondered if I was fooling myself. We still didn't come to a compromise on my record label, and I was still solid in not wanting to follow in my father's footsteps. Somehow, there was something about Marcello and the way I felt about him that made me feel as though we could change the trajectory of the family business and make it worthwhile to stay. On the other hand, I wondered if he had just swooned me into thinking we would have a great life that we could build together just to placate me until our marriage was official. *Why am I like this? Why do I assume the worst?*

"Jesus, there should be a flash warning with that thing," Harper teased as she came into the kitchen and poured herself some coffee, breaking me out of my thoughts.

"What are you talking about?"

"That huge rock on your finger," she chuckled, pointing to my engagement ring as she sat next to me. "I may have to go get my sunglasses."

"Shut up," I snorted as I turned my hand to admire the new jewelry. It really was ridiculous.

"Are you seriously going to keep that thing? It doesn't fit you, and it's too big to be functional."

"I don't know," I pondered. "It is beautiful, but you're right. It's totally not my style."

"You're going to keep it, aren't you?"

"I've worn it for two days, Harper. It'll take time to get used to it. If it's too much, Marcello will exchange it. It's no big deal." Harper stared at me in confusion. "What?"

"You're speaking as though you have months to wear it and figure out if you like it and not as though we are leaving in three days. Keep it and pawn it."

Shit, shit, shit! Harper stayed at Jacobs the day after Marc proposed, and we hadn't spoken until now. She had no idea I was thinking of staying, but I couldn't bring myself to tell her just yet.

"I'm not pawning it, Harper. But I will be expected to wear it until the wedding, so I'm just trying to get used to it."

Harper studied me a moment longer before letting it go. She knew something was off with me but decided against saying anything. I could tell by the way she looked at me. I was thankful she let it go, though. I was a terrible liar, and I wasn't sure I would be able to keep myself from blabbing if she kept asking questions. I knew she would support me no matter what, but she had been raving about New

York, and I didn't want to break her heart about not going.

My phone pinged from the living room, and I was grateful for the distraction to leave the kitchen. Harper dropped the subject of my ring, but there was still a layer of tension lingering between us, and I needed it to disappear. When I grabbed my phone, my heart palpitated as I saw there was a text from Marc.

Be ready in 30. We're going on a quick trip.

We just got back from a quick trip.

Where did he want to take me now? It seemed odd that he wanted to take another mini vacay when we were getting married in three days and would then be leaving for our honeymoon.

This one is to somewhere warmer. Pack your suit and sunscreen. See you soon.

Do I not get a say in this?

Of course, I wouldn't turn down a tropical getaway, but I wanted to make him sweat just a little. He was a little too comfortable with ordering me around.

Are you turning down Costa Rica?

Holy crap! Costa Rica? Keep it cool, Mila.

Meh. I think that place is overrated.

I started to pace the floor, waiting for the three small dots to quit moving. I was nervous and excited at the same time. I loved to push Marc when he was used to getting what he wanted. He was the type of man that was never told no and dominated every aspect of his life and those in it. I loved challenging that but knew I was playing with fire. I bit my thumbnail, waiting for him to respond.

Instead of answering my text, he responded with a photo that stopped me in my tracks, leaving my mouth hanging wide open. He sent me a photo of his reflection in a mirror that showed he was nude and fully erect, his hand gripping his cock. A text followed shortly after, and I had to tear my eyes away from the glorious explicit image on my phone.

This is what I plan to wear while on our trip. Are you sure you want to stay behind?

See you in twenty minutes.

"What's got you drooling like a canine?" Harper asked from the kitchen doorway.

"Marcello just invited me to Costa Rica. He's going to be here shortly."

"That's doesn't explain the drool."

I clicked my tongue as I tried to decide if I would tell her what he sent me. I was sure she and Jacob sent similar photos to one another, but I suddenly felt protective of Marc. I knew she would ask to see the photo, and I could never do that.

"He showed me his new suit, and he looks fine as hell," I lied. Well, sort of.

"Mhm," she smirked before padding to her bedroom.

I followed behind to pack a bag. He didn't say how long we would be gone, but I figured it wouldn't be any longer than the Lake Tahoe trip with our wedding so close. I threw in a yellow bikini along with a light, floral dress in case we went out. Harper came in and sat on the edge of my bed as I continued to gather the rest of my necessities.

"Don't forget the objective, Mila."

"What do you mean?"

"I mean, we are leaving in two days, and you're starting to give the impression that you're actually starting to fall for Marcello. You know, the man keeping you from opening your music label. The man you're being arranged to marry and that you'll be thrown right into the life you've wanted nothing to do with."

"He's not a bad guy, Harper. He's actually really sweet."

"What about the rest?"

"Don't worry, we're still going to New York. I'm just starting to wonder if things would be different if I hadn't turned my back on everything. It feels like there could be a lot of potential with Marcello."

"Mila," Harper grabbed my hand so that I would give her my full attention. "If you're having second thoughts you need to tell me."

"I'm good, Harper," I assured her. I couldn't tell her otherwise, like a coward. I was still so confused. I needed more time to think about everything, but time wasn't on my side with the wedding only three days away our plans to leave in two. "We'll be out of here in two days, as planned."

Harper scowled as she observed me. I continued with the task of packing, doing my best to act as though I wasn't being torn in two on the inside as I avoided making eye contact so that she didn't see it. Perhaps this trip would finalize my decision once and for all.

Within forty minutes, I was at the hanger for the second time in one week, walking with Marcello to their private plane. He was quiet on the ride over, which seemed odd. There was an uneasy feeling that I couldn't put my finger on. As we boarded, I was surprised to see the cabin full this time, including my father and two of his men. There was also Marcello's father, Dante and Dominic, and a couple of other men I didn't know. No one paid attention to the fact that we had joined them, and Marcello sat with me for a moment as we took off.

"What is this?" I quietly hissed to Marc.

"What do you mean?" His voice was void of any emotion whatsoever.

"Why the hell is everyone here? I thought we were getting away for an evening."

"I never said it would be just the two of us," Marcello answered dryly.

It was as if he needed to remain stoic and made of stone in front of his men and my father. He was completely different from our Lake Tahoe trip, making me feel less secure in my recent revelations of how I felt for him and that I was considering staying. "Shit." He was so cold and distant, and I hated it.

"Need I remind you of the photo you sent me of your new suit?" I used air quotes to add emphasis to the end of my sentence.

Marcello rolled his eyes and smirked as he set his gaze out of the small window next to him. Anger rose from my belly. I could feel my cheeks redden, and it wasn't from being turned on. Why was he being such an ass all of the sudden? I thought we were past this. I could feel eyes on me, and when I looked for the source of my unease, I found my father talking closely with his two men, who were all looking at me. I already regretted the trip, and it was only fifteen minutes after take-off. I tried to be silent and give Marcello time to collect himself and realize how he was acting, but I couldn't keep my mouth shut. This trip looked as though it revolved around business in some way, and I wanted nothing to do with it.

I glared at my father before turning my body enough so that I was facing Marcello, and, hopefully, getting a touch of privacy with my back toward him.

"You need to talk to me, Marcello." I saw my future

husband flinch at my voice and felt like I was slapped. *What the hell?*

"About what, *Mila*?"

Why did he say my name like that? "Is this a business trip, and you just forgot to tell me? Why is everyone here?"

"I was just taken captive, and the men are worried about my — our — safety while we leave the country. Stop worrying so much and enjoy the trip."

"I swear, Marcello, if this has anything to do with any kind of business between our families, I'll—"

"You'll what?" He bit out in a whisper, cutting me off. He looked around to make sure he hadn't caught anyone else's attention before he continued. "Trips like this will be part of our everyday lives, so get used to them. Everyone here knows you want nothing to do with it, so you'll stay out of the way. Sit back, relax, and enjoy the beach."

Marc unbuckled his seatbelt and moved to sit with his father and men, not saying another word, leaving me dumbfounded and pissed off. He was like Jackyl and Hyde, and I didn't like it. What happened for him to change so completely in the course of two days? The Marcello on the plane was the version I had heard about here and there, the monster I vowed to never have anything to do with. I felt nauseous.

I got up to use the bathroom but was pulled aside by one of my father's men.

"Your father would like a word," he said.

"I'm sure he would. Unfortunately for him, I only have the capacity to deal with one controlling asshole today and, surprisingly, I've already met my quota."

"Sit down, Mila," my father ground out through clenched teeth.

I rolled my eyes and plopped down on the seat

between my father and Hector, his right hand. Hector offered an apologetic smile, knowing my relationship with my father wasn't the best. He was a tall, rough looking guy with a scar from his hairline all the way down to his chin. He reminded me more of a biker than mafia muscle and acted like one too. He was rough on the outside when he needed to be, but he had a soft side to him that he wasn't afraid to show to those he was close to. He was one of the most loyal people I had ever met. When I was younger, he would always try to find ways to make me laugh or to keep me occupied enough to not pay attention to what was going on around us.

"You need to remember who you are right now and act accordingly," my father ordered. "You being here is a huge risk and mistake that Marcello will have to deal with the consequences of later. Until we get back, you need to act like you are *my* daughter. No bullshit."

"Stop treating me like a child," I said angrily, trying my best not to lose my cool or raise my voice.

"Then don't act like one," my father retorted. "You need to show you can be the wife Marcello needs during a time like this and that your own issues with our family won't bleed into our dealings. We need to show a united front. Do not screw this up, Mila."

"If nothing else, just stick to the hut and enjoy the sun and the water," Hector added, trying to alleviate the stress.

I glared at my father, beyond upset that he basically told me to behave as though I were an adolescent, proving once more why I wanted to have nothing to do with any of this life. I refused to spend the rest of my years being ordered around by my father and men like him. I knew how important my marriage to Marcello was, and I realized that, deep down, I wanted to present myself in the best way for Marc, but I refused to tuck tail and obey where my father was concerned.

I smiled sweetly at my father, knowing good and well he would know I was up to no good, but I was past the point of being willing to please anyone but myself. And at that moment, I wanted to lose my fucking mind. But being in a small, enclosed space with no exit, I landed on getting drunk. As the stewardess passed by, I asked her for three tequila shots. She looked at my father as if to ask for his permission, and it pissed me off even more.

"I don't need my daddy's permission to have a couple drinks, okay? Three tequila shots, please. Now."

I hated being curt with the woman — she was only doing her job. I was sure someone had told her to monitor my drinking, and that thought really made me want to act out of character. My father thought I was an irresponsible child, and I had half a mind to act like one. Although, I was on a plane with my future husband, along with his father and brothers, so I figured it would be best to just stick to slightly drunken me and not give two shits. I was tired of being torn into two different directions, and I desperately wanted a moment to just *be*.

CHAPTER
THIRTEEN
MILA

I RETURNED to my original seat and downed all three shots the moment the stewardess set them in front of me. Before she walked away, I asked her to turn on dance music and to crank it up. When she started to protest, I assured her, in my sweetest sarcastic voice, that it would be best if she didn't deny my request.

I thought my father would wait until I was married before he forced this shit on me. Of course, we were only three days away, so why wait? Marcello's attitude and shift in character around me made things worse. He knew I didn't want anything to do with this side of our families business, and I truly thought we would be able to work out some kind of compromise or under-standing and that he wanted to make it work for us to be together. But from the looks of things, he had decided to follow my father's lead without protest.

Letting the alcohol get absorbed into my system, I swayed to the music playing through the speakers. I could hear murmurs from opposite ends of the cabin, but no one attempted to have the music turned down, which disappointed me. I was ready for a fight. When the stewardess walked by again, I asked for one more shot and for her to turn the music up louder. Was I being petty? Abso-fucking-lutely.

My body warmed and buzzed with my fourth tequila, and a song I loved came on. I shot out of my seat and started dancing in the middle of the cabin of the plane. I didn't care how anyone saw me; I was letting the music move me. I closed my eyes and swayed my hips to the beat, getting completely lost in the moment. I felt two large hands on my hips as someone approached me from behind. I didn't think twice about it being anyone other than Marcello. No one would be that dumb.

"You can shake that ass for me any time, sweet cheeks," a deep raspy voice commented in my ear, and chills ran down my spine. That voice did not belong to Marc, or anyone else I knew for that matter.

Before I could turn to see who it was, Marcello was there, snatching him by the back of the neck. He punched the man square in the nose, instantly drawing blood. There was no way it wasn't broken. I watched with wide eyes as Marc made the man stand straight, and he held him in place with his large hand wrapped around his neck.

"Touch her again, and you'll be tossed off this plane without a fucking parachute," Marcello growled at his father's man.

"Sorry, boss. I...I didn't mean any disrespect," the guy stammered as he held his hands in front of himself as if to fend off Marcello, letting the blood flow from his nose and down his chin.

"You're mine, bella. No one touches what's mine." Marc took my hand and yanked me to the back of the cabin with force. I couldn't stop myself from going with him — he was too strong. He stopped abruptly when we came up to his father. "Teach your men their place and how to fucking act," he spit out before continuing to a small bedroom, where he closed the door behind us, his breath labored.

"What the hell was that, Mila?" he spat out.

"Why are you yelling at me? I was just dancing."

"You were making a scene, and you know it. You were trying to get a rise out of me," he barked. "Quit playing games."

I clenched my hands into fists and felt a fire in my soul, fueled by four tequila shots and anger.

"Contrary to belief, I don't make every decision with you in mind!" That was a lie. "You and my father are forcing me into some sort of business dealing I know nothing about, nor do I want to. You know I want nothing to do with this, yet you bring me along anyway under the guise of us having a quick romantic getaway."

"I never said it was a romantic getaway!"

"You implied it!" I yelled as loud as I could. I didn't care if he saw my anger, and I didn't care if everyone on the other side of the small bedroom door could hear us. "You weren't forthcoming with what this trip was about, and then you reverted back to the asshole bossy prince I never wanted anything to do with in the first place! So, who's playing games, huh? Did you figure you could win me over after one sweet weekend together, then go back to business as usual as if nothing we talked about mattered?"

Despite my effort to stop them, tears fell from my eyes. I was so charged with emotion that I didn't even know if I was hurt or just plain pissed off. I guess it didn't matter. Marcello's face softened, and his demeanor loosened as he took a step toward me. I couldn't decide if I wanted him near me or not. I wasn't in the mood to fight anymore, but I didn't want to be close to Marc if he was going to continue being the prince of assholes that had walked onto the plane.

I wiped my tears away and looked at my feet as I gathered myself. I didn't notice Marc had stepped right in front of me when he lifted my chin up to his face and kissed me. At first, I welcomed the familiar feeling of his lips to mine, but I snapped out of it quickly. I reared back and smacked him across the face. The second I did it, I covered my mouth with my hands in surprise at what I'd done. The look of shock on his face would stay with me for quite some time. *Holy shit, did I just smack him? Ohmygod, ohmygod, ohmygod.*

My mind raced for a way to take it back, but I realized I didn't want to take it back. He deserved it for how he had treated me. I'd never smacked anyone and wasn't violent by nature. It twisted my belly that I had put my hands on him, but I didn't want to appear weak. My father was Don Aleksander Fedorov. Would it really be that surprising that his daughter would slap someone for being rude and disrespectful? He was known for gaining respect by force. Then again, I wanted nothing to do with that. It was one reason I hated being who I was. But no matter what I was feeling, I refused to let Marcello take control of the situation. Without another thought, I dropped to my knees and started unfastening his pants.

"Mila," he urged calmly, trying to get my attention as he attempted to stop my advance.

I slapped his hand out of the way and yanked his pants down along with his boxers. I was shocked to see he was partially hard. *He likes this? Of course, he does.*

We didn't have much room to maneuver about the space. The queen-sized bed took up the majority of the room, and the door and the small closet were to my back. Not wanting him on the bed to give him any sort of advantage to shift the hands of control, I decided to just go for it as he stood.

I looked up at his confused expression as I grasped his hardening cock and took him in my mouth, sucking him fast and hard. He instantly leaned forward to brace his hands against the door that was behind me.

"Jesus, bella," was all he could get out before I nipped the sensitive tip of his dick with my teeth. "Fuck," he growled.

I continued to suck him off with purpose, never slowing down for a moment. I could feel he was getting harder in my mouth and wondered if he was getting close. But I didn't have to wonder long.

"Dam, Mila," he breathed as he tried to hold on as long as he could.

Wanting to make him realize I was pissed and hurt, I made a split-second decision to play a card from his own deck. I gave him one final suck, then let him plop out of my mouth before he could finish. I stood, wiped the corners of my mouth, and smiled wide.

"This isn't funny, Mila," he bit out.

"Oh, I know," I responded before leaving him alone in the small bedroom with his pants around his ankles, pulling the door closed behind me.

The rest of the flight wasn't eventful as Marcello sulked with his brothers, and Hector managed to keep my father off my back. Now and again, I felt Marcello's father, Antonio, staring me down. I wondered why he would study me, and I hated being under the scrutiny of two patriarchs.

When we landed, I welcomed the sun and the warmth. The cabin was getting stuffy, and the air was electrified with the tension between everyone. There were three heavily tinted SUVs waiting for us, and Marcello quickly guided me to the closest vehicle. We slid in the back as Dante and one of the other DeLuca men slid into the front seats. I watched my father, Hector, and their guard, pile into the second car and the rest took up the rear vehicle.

"Where's Shane?" I couldn't believe I hadn't noticed Shane was missing until we were five hours away from home.

"He stayed back to deal with some things with Cristiano," Marc answered.

"Are we not good enough for you, Mila?" Dante asked from the passenger seat.

"I guess you'll do," I teased, earning a smile from Marcello's brother.

When I looked over to Marc, he had his mirrored shades on and was looking out of the window. *Is he pouting?*

"Are you pouting?" I leaned in to ask Marc, trying not to laugh.

How ridiculous was it to think of Marcello DeLuca pouting because he was put in his place by little ol' me. Okay, I kind of loved it. He just turned and glared at me...I think. I could only see my own reflection in his shades, along with a slight furrow of his dark brows and the thin, tight line of his lips.

I let out an awkward sound as the laugh I was holding broke free. "Holy shit, you are! Oh, come on, Marc. It's nothing you haven't done to me."

"That's different," he answered.

"How?"

He just looked at me for a moment, then turned

back to the window without answering. No way was he about to tell me it was okay for him to leave me hanging but not the other way around. We were equals, and I would make sure he saw that, especially in the bedroom. I didn't push the issue, but I did want to bridge the gap between us.

The scenery outside was beautiful, and I wasn't in the mood to fight any longer. Especially if this could be our last night together, I wanted it to be memorable in a good way. I took a deep breath and slid my hand into Marcello's. He didn't look at me, but he didn't take his hand away either. Maybe he was struggling the same as I was.

After a little over an hour, the driver announced we had arrived at Tamarindo. Marcello and I were led to an adorable second floor bungalow that was close to the water. There was an entire wall open on the side of our rental, where a large hammock hung next to a full-sized bed. There were also a small kitchenette and table overlooking the view of the water. It was magical.

"Do you want to swim?" Marcello asked.

"Will you be joining me?"

"Yes, though I think it's best I wear some shorts, yeah?"

I smiled at the over six-foot tall handsome Italian grinning at me. *Finally, he's being more himself.* He walked over to me and pulled me into his arms.

"I'm sorry, bella. I know I was a dick on the plane. This was a last-minute trip, and I was hoping you being here would make it more enjoyable, but I may have misjudged that a little."

"I just need you to be more forthcoming with me. Tell me what's going on. We will never work if you're always keeping secrets."

"How can I not keep secrets when you don't want

this life?" He gently moved a strand of hair out of my face and caressed my cheek with his thumb.

"We will find a way to find balance, but not if you continue on like this morning."

"You weren't on your best behavior either," he playfully scolded.

"Well, that was more about my father, but then your cold shoulder sent me over the edge."

"How about we go spend the rest of the day in the ocean and wash all that off us?" he suggested with a kiss to my forehead, making me smile wider and nod fanatically.

We spent the rest of the day doing exactly that. We laid out in the sun and swam together in the beautiful crystal clear water. Marc was back to his sweet, fun self until the day started to come to an end. I had asked what was on his mind, but he assured me all was well. After eight, we returned to our bungalow to shower and dress for dinner. He was taking me to a local place that was tucked away and known for its incredible food.

The tropical restaurant had patio seatings on three sides of the building, with lights strewn overhead, and an outdoor bar. Inside, there was another larger bar and tables all around, with tropical, island themed décor. I loved every bit of it.

"This is perfect," I gushed as we were seated on the patio area toward the front of the building.

As I looked around, I noticed the men from both families spread out through the restaurant, but they acted as though they didn't know one another. Marcello's brothers were nowhere in sight, and neither were our fathers. I had an odd feeling about the evening but brushed it off when Marcello happily went over all of the great, local food on the menu.

When our meal was just ending, Dante walked up to our table and whispered something into Marcello's ear.

"I'll be right back, bella," Marc said as he wiped his mouth with his napkin and got up.

The men walked away cool and collected, but my gut was telling me something was wrong. I peeked around the other tables and diners to try and see if I could see where they had gone off to, but they were nowhere to be seen. I sat awkwardly, waiting for Marc to come back for about twenty minutes. When I saw him and Dante coming toward me, they were walking a touch faster than before. Their calm energy was disturbed, even though they tried to hide it.

"Let's go, Mila," Marcello ordered, hardly stopping to make sure I was getting out of my seat.

My heart jumped in my throat with worry about what was happening. Marcello took my hand in his and quickly led us out and to the vehicles, Dante right behind us. When we reached the SUV, I heard a scuffle and then people screaming.

"Get in, now," Dante barked.

I didn't ask questions. I jumped into the back seat with Marc as Dante slid into the driver's seat. The passenger door opened, making me scream. I felt like an idiot when one of Marc's men hopped in.

"Relax, Mila. We're alright," Marcello whispered in my ear as he wrapped an arm around me.

As our car rounded to leave, I saw our other two SUVs and our fathers being rushed into them. Our small convoy pulled onto the road just as authorities were pulling in.

"What happened back there, Marcello?"

"Nothing, bella. That wasn't us," he answered, pointing back toward the restaurant.

"Then why were you and Dante rushing out?" I wanted to believe him. We had just talked about him keeping secrets, but my intuition wouldn't let me leave it alone.

"We saw a fight break out and wanted to get out of there. That's also why our fathers left so quickly. We don't need to be any part of that nonsense."

He sounded so honest and reassuring, I decided to let it go, even though I could tell he was lying. I had been around my father enough when I was younger to know that we had everything to do with what happened back there. I was reminded of why I wanted to get as far away from my family as possible. I couldn't marry Marcello when he was clearly in too deep to do anything other than how he was taught. Yes, I loved him fiercely, but I couldn't stay. I needed to make the best decision for myself, and that was New York. I just needed one more night with him to take the memory with me when I left.

CHAPTER
FOURTEEN
MARCELLO

I HATED LYING TO MILA. After Lake Tahoe, I truly wanted to start something new and find a way for her to fit into my life in Los Angeles. I knew she wanted nothing to do with our legacy, but I was making positive changes that I thought she would be proud of and would see there was space for her to be happy. My father might not have been open to change at first, but he had told me he was happy to see me taking the initiative for our business to evolve with the generations. I just needed the Don to retire so that I had more freedom to do what I planned, but I needed Mila by my side. Not just because of who her father was, but because she gave me hope for the future and for a life where we could have children of our own and let them decide their own fate.

When I received word that the Don wanted Mila and I to travel to Costa Rica with them, my heart sank. I knew exactly why he wanted us there, but I wasn't in a position to tell him no. There was a family in Costa Rica that was trying to push their own agenda through our channels of business, potentially leading to us being exposed and have connections to illegal activity we have moved away from decades ago. I knew there was potential for the trip to go south, which led me to being in a shit mood. I wanted to shield Mila from that kind of drama, but her father felt she needed the exposure.

I was only a witness to our father's doings, but I wanted Mila far away from the windfall, so I got her away from the restaurant as fast as possible. I knew she would have questions, but I wasn't ready to give them to her, which left me with no other option but to lie for the sake of her safety. I held her tight as we made our way back to the bungalow. She was quiet and seemed to be in her own head about something, which worried me. I could feel a distance between us. I knew she had to be upset about being thrown into this situation, but I thought I could make her see my side of things if she just heard me out. We had made so much progress, and I fucked it all up by not standing my ground to her father and refused her to accompany us. It didn't help that I reverted to my usual, closed-off self. I needed to feel close to Mila and for her to know I was still with her. That I still wanted to marry her and build our lives around her dreams as well as mine.

"Give us some privacy," I told Dante as we got out of the SUV when we arrived back to the bungalow.

"That's not a good idea, brother."

"You can stay in the car and watch our door. That's the only way in. But I need some time with Mila without distractions or eavesdropping."

"Fine," Dante agreed with a huff. "Whatever you say," he said with a slap on the back.

I knew he hated to leave me even a little unprotected, but I knew I could handle myself if anything happened. I was caught off guard when Bruno attacked me. That wouldn't happen again.

"How do you feel about a night swim?" I asked Mila as I walked her to our rental.

"Sure," she answered quietly.

"I promise, everything is okay."

"I know. I'm just getting tired," she admitted. "But a night swim sounds perfect."

With a smile, I grabbed her hand and led her to the water instead of our room. As we approached the beach, there was a stand of towels, and I picked two up for us. I was happy to see that we had the area all to ourselves. When we came to a lounge chair close to the water's edge, I stopped and started taking off my socks and shoes.

"What are you doing?" Mila asked as she looked around to make sure we weren't seen.

"I'm taking my clothes off," I laughed as I pulled my shirt over my head and tossed it at her.

"I can see that," she chuckled. "I thought we agreed on wearing swimsuits while we were here."

"Nah. I want to see my breathtakingly beautiful princess standing in the ocean with the moonlight as her spotlight."

"You're so cheesy," she snorted.

She kicked off her sandals and pulled her floral dress over her head. Then she stood before me in a white lace see-through bra and matching panties. I stood and admired her in the moonlight, forging the memory into my brain.

"You're staring," she teased.

"I'm admiring perfection," I corrected before removing the rest of my clothes.

I stepped up to Mila and lightly rubbed her arms. I kissed her gently as I caressed the sides of her breasts with my fingertips, barely touching the fabric covering the sensitive skin. She slid her arms around my middle and pulled me closer. I took my time to kiss her skin as I removed her bra. She stepped out of her panties and tossed them onto the lounge chair beside us. Without having to say a word, we told one another how we felt with our hands and our lips.

I slowly pulled Mila back into the water until we were waist deep. The water was perfect as it quietly lapped around us. I brushed my thumbs over Mila's hard nipples, making her shiver.

"It's so beautiful here," she whispered, but she wasn't looking at the scenery. She was looking at me. Mila was angelic, standing in the water under the moonlight.

"You're beautiful, bella," I whispered back before kissing her, this time with more passion.

She wound her arms around my neck and jumped up with a wave just as I moved my hands to grab her ass. I helped her wrap her legs around my waist, deepening our kiss. I let go of all the tension from the day, instantly feeling safe in her arms, knowing I could be myself with her. I walked us a little closer to the beach so that I could sit with her straddling me while still being in the water. I needed to be closer to her. To feel her.

Mila feathered my neck with kisses as I slid two fingers into her sweet pussy, ecstatic to find that she was already wet for me.

"I love that you're always ready for me, bella," I breathed into her ear. She moaned in response as I worked my fingers inside her for a moment.

"I need you," she moaned. She didn't need to say it twice.

I removed my fingers and helped her as she settled over my erect cock. We looked into each other's eyes, and she slid herself into place. I thrusted deeper into her, making her head fall back. I kissed the exposed flesh as she moved her hips, setting the rhythm. Rocking faster, she leaned back, just enough for her hands to rest on my thighs for support. The sight of her supple breasts moving with her as she rode my cock in the ocean was a memory I would have forever. It felt like a dream.

I could feel her walls starting to close tighter, letting me know she was getting close. I wanted to finish with her but still let her keep control of our pace, so I leaned forward to grab the back of her neck and gently pull her back to me. I kissed her full lips as I leaned back to a laying position, grateful for the water being so shallow where we were. She instantly started to bounce and rock, bringing herself closer and closer to orgasm. Then she lifted herself to her knees and quickly bounced herself up and down on the head of my cock, driving me crazy.

"Fuck, Mila, cum with me," I groaned, digging my fingers into her flesh.

She moaned as she bounced faster, resting most of her weight on her forearms on either side of my head. Suddenly, she dropped herself all the way down and started rocking, sending me over the edge. We both yelled out for each other as we came together, tightening and convulsing with the intensity of our lovemaking.

"I love you so damn much, Mila," I whispered into her ear as we laid in the water, letting the water lap over us as we got our breathing and heart rates under control.

I thought I heard her sniffle, so I quickly adjusted

myself to see her face. My heart dipped when I saw tears streaming down her face.

"What's wrong my love?"

"Nothing. This was just such a beautiful night. I love you, Marcello."

We lost track of time as we laid in one another's arms, listening to the calming waves. When we were both yawning, we decided to grab our clothes and head back to the bungalow for bed. I fell asleep with Mila tight in my arms. That night, I realized that I would do anything for her. That she had secretly moved to a place in my heart from where she would never be able to leave. She would always be with me, no matter what. She was my world, and I felt a strong need to not only protect her, but also to make all her dreams come true.

Mila

I woke just before dawn, grateful that Marcello was still asleep. I slid out from his arms and tiptoed to the bathroom to pee. When I came back out, he was snoring, letting me know he was in a deep sleep.

It's now or never, Mila.

With tears in my eyes, I quickly dressed and gathered my things, careful not to wake my sleeping prince. The way we had made love in the ocean tore at my heart, knowing I was planning to leave. I had felt him opening up to me all the way, which made this so much harder. I loved him deeply but could not live my life as a mafia princess. I didn't want it. And no matter how much I loved Marc, he would never turn his back on the only life he had ever known. I had no choice. I had to leave.

I took one last look at Marcello, naked and asleep like a Roman god. He looked so peaceful. I blew him a kiss before slipping out of the bungalow. I spotted the SUVs parked and peeked inside. The first two were empty, but Hector and his man were in the third.

"Is everything alright, Mila?" Hector asked as I approached the vehicle with my bag.

"I need to leave. Now," I answered as I got into the backseat. "Where's my father?"

"He's sleeping. Should I wake him?"

"No. He can leave with the others, but I can't wait. I need to get home. Where are the DeLuca's men?"

"They are all asleep. It's our watch."

"Good, then we need to leave before they wake."

The men looked at one another, not sure what to think of the situation. "We need to check with the Don," the driver finally said to Hector.

"Who are you to question me?" I snapped. "What's your name anyway?"

"Brian," he answered, eyeing me through the rear-view mirror.

"Well, Brian, when you work for my father, you also work for me. If I tell you we need to leave, you say okay, and get us the hell out of here."

"Let's go," Hector said after a brief silence.

Brian gave him one last look before giving in and pulling away from the resort. Hector arranged a flight home for me, and I made sure Harper would be home when I arrived. The moment I saw her as I walked into our apartment, I broke down and cried in her arms. I told her how Marcello had changed so much and how I had fallen for him. I told her that even though I felt the way I did, the night in Costa Rica proved I wasn't made for that life and that I needed to leave. I wouldn't sacrifice my happiness, even though I loved Marc so deeply. We both agreed it would be easier to open my music label in another city anyway, away from both the DeLuca and Fedorov families.

I spent the rest of the evening packing and planning our route for the next night. I also avoided calls and texts from Marcello. I hoped he wouldn't come over but banked on him to come looking for me. I hoped he would assume I just needed some space before our wedding and that he would never question whether or not I would leave.

That night, I cried myself to sleep, already mourning the loss of my first love. I knew I was making the right choice to leave, but it was hard as hell. I slept most of the next day, managing to convince Anya that I would meet her at the bar for my bachelorette party. It was close to eight the night before my wedding Jacob came to pick us up.

"Hey, babe. So, you know where to meet me later?" Harper asked Jacob as she put on her shoes and grabbed her purse. She was dressed to go out and her bags were nowhere in sight.

"Where are you going? We're leaving." I started to panic. I didn't want to leave without my best friend.

"Jacob and I were talking earlier, and he made a good point. We need to get away without raising suspicion. So, we thought it would be best if I went to the bachelorette party to make an appearance. Then, when everyone asks where you are, I will leave to go look for you when, really, I will be heading to you and Jacob."

"Where will we be? I don't want to hang around LA waiting for you. We need to make some good time before the morning."

"There is a diner that is open all night about two hours from here," Jacob answered. "We will head there and wait for Harper. It's not by the main highway, so we should still be able to slip away."

I looked at my friend with a worried look. "Oh, it'll work out perfectly, you'll see," Harper assured me.

She gave me a tight squeeze, then left for my bachelorette party. Jacob and I loaded our things into his car and headed to the diner. He had given me an idea of the general direction of where the diner was, so I was confused when he took a turn, driving us in the opposite direction.

"Wait, aren't we supposed to go that way?" I asked him.

He kept his eyes forward and didn't respond. *What the fuck?*

"Jacob," I said louder to get his attention. "What's happening? You're going the wrong way."

My heart felt like it would beat out of my chest. I felt nauseous, fearing the worst. There was no way Jacob would betray Harper. He loved her, right?

"Change of plans, bitch," Jacob gritted out before slamming my head against the window, and everything went black.

CHAPTER
FIFTEEN
MARCELLO

THE SUN WAS WARMING my face as I began to wake, searching the bed for Mila. When my hands met the empty mattress, I opened my eyes and looked around the small bungalow for her. Not seeing her, I stepped into my shorts and headed to the water to see if she was sunbathing. When I didn't see her, I began to worry. *Were we careful enough last night? Did they follow us back?*

I hurried back up the beach to find my brothers. They weren't in their room or in the SUV, so I looked at the small café attached to the resort and found them all sitting at a table in a heated discussion.

"Why the hell isn't anyone on watch?" I demanded as I took a seat at the table. Everyone fell silent and looked at each other. "Speak!" My anger was rising, and I didn't care. Mila was missing, and there was obviously something that had the men uneasy. As I looked around the table, I realized the Don was there, but Hector and Brian were gone. *Maybe she went shopping with her father's men and just forgot to tell me.*

"Hector and Brian are gone," the Don answered from the other side of the table.

"Gone where?" I asked.

"We don't know," my father piped in. "They didn't say a word to anyone. They left sometime before sunrise."

"What about Mila?" I asked, squeezing my hands into fists as tight as possible. I felt like punching someone. *Where the fuck is Mila?*

"We all figured she was with you," Dominic answered. "You know, turn that water action into some hammock action." He stuck his tongue to his cheek and winked, proud of his joke and not registering my level of anger.

"You were fucking watching?" I boomed as I stood up, sending my chair across the floor behind me. Dante instantly rose to keep me away from our little brother.

"Relax, man," Dominic continued with ease. "We were on watch, and you *did* choose a very public place to—" He was cut off when Dante smacked him upside his head.

"Learn when to shut up, stupido," Dante warned.

"Are you telling me none of you saw Hector, Brian, or Mila leave?" I boomed so the whole table could hear me. Shit, the entire cafe heard me.

"Shit, you don't think..." Dominic started but didn't continue his thought.

"Think what?"

"Well, after last night, are we sure everyone went their separate ways?"

"Those cowards would never dare to touch my daughter," the Don answered. "Knowing Mila, she ran."

Murmurs filled the table. *Ran? She wouldn't do that. She loves me.*

"Why would she do that? We had a deal, Aleksander," my father bit out, banging his fist on the table. "How the fuck have you managed to run all your businesses effortlessly, but you can't control your daughters? Have you never taught them respect? Their responsibility to their family!?"

"You remember who you're speaking to, Antonio," the Don responded slowly and calmly, with a hint of ice and warning.

"Shit," Dante muttered under his breath beside me.

My father stood, and the others followed. "You get a leash on that daughter, Fedorov, and she better be at that alter in two days."

My father stomped off with his men in tow. Dante and Dominic stayed behind with me and the Don. I was trying to wrap my head around Mila leaving along with our families now on edge with the threat of our alliance falling. *How did this happen?*

"I thought you two were good," Dante hissed.

"You better find my daughter, Marcello. She is your responsibility, so I will give you that chance to correct this grave mistake. If you fail to bring my daughter back, I will step in, and no one will like my tactics."

The Don rose from his chair as a picture of composure and power. I knew how dangerous and malicious he could be, and I didn't want any of that falling on my Mila.

"Go with Aleksander and make sure everything is ready to go with the plane," I ordered Dominic, who obeyed without question.

When it was only Dante and I left, I dropped into a chair.

"What the hell, Marcello?"

"I don't know, Dante. Everything was so perfect last night. I knew she was upset about the possibility that we were here for business, but after dinner, we were good. I had no idea she wanted to leave."

"Do you want her back?"

"What kind of question is that?"

"An honest one. Is it worth the trouble to find her and bring her back? Especially if she's willing to betray her own father to get away from this life? Who's to say she doesn't run the second we bring her back?"

"I love her, Dante. I will find her, and then find a way to make her want to stay. Everything will crumble if we don't get married."

"So, it's still all about the alliance?"

"Yes," I answered annoyed. "No — I don't know what to do here, Dante. I know that we can't have unrest between us and the Fedorovs. Too much is at stake. But more than that, I don't want to be without Mila. She's ruined me in the best possible way."

"You sound like a sad, lovesick puppy," Dante teased, and I glared at him in response. "Fine, then go get your girl. I'll hold things down between the dads and keep a war from breaking out."

I stood and pulled my brother into a tight hug. "Thanks, bro. I know I can always count on you."

"But Marc," he warned as he looked me straight in the eyes. "You don't have a lot of time. Get Mila home."

I called and texted Mila on our flight home, not missing the glares between my father and hers. The tension could be cut with a knife, and my anxiety about Mila didn't help anything. I called all of my men, including Shane and Cristiano, and had them looking for Mila. I even reached out to George Martin to make sure that slob didn't have anything to do with her leaving me in the dead of night.

A part of me wondered if she just needed time to be sure of what she wanted before our wedding day, but she would have told me if that was it. Our night had been perfect, and I told her how much I loved her. I couldn't believe she would just leave.

I paced the floor of my suite, waiting for any word from Mila or from my men about her whereabouts. Anya had told me Harper showed up to Mila's bachelorette party, but Mila never showed up. When Anya grew concerned for her sister, she sent Harper looking for her but never heard anything more.

"Where the hell are you, bella?"

Mila

I groaned as I opened my eyes, and my head was throbbing. I looked around me but could hardly see anything. All I could gather was that I was in some kind of shack or rundown cabin. The floor was wooden, and the only piece of furniture I could see was a broken, tattered couch and a dusty dresser with a drawer missing.

My hands were bound behind me, and my ankles too. It was still dark outside, but I couldn't hear any signs of cars or indicators that we were anywhere near the city.

Harper must be freaking out.

"Hello!" I yelled out into the dark, hoping someone would answer. "Help! Someone please help me!"

Why would Jacob do this? Why would he take me?

The door suddenly opened, and a large shadow hid behind the bright light of an electric lantern. A pale, yellow light filled the room behind him, where I could hear others talking and joking around.

"No one will hear you out here, Mila Fedorov."

"Who the hell are you? Where's Jacob? What is this?"

"So many questions," the man said as he came closer.

He squatted in front of me, setting the lantern to the side. He couldn't be much older than Marcello and looked vaguely familiar. In normal circumstances, I would think he was an attractive guy, but in the shadowed light, he looked menacing.

"Don't worry about Jacob. His job is done."

"Why the fuck did he do this?"

"He's got a little vendetta against your future husband, much like me. He was our way to get to you."

"A fucking mole!? Are you kidding me? Did he even care about Harper?" I asked, not really expecting a response. I fought against my restraints, only managing to hurt my wrists more.

"Who cares?"

I glared at the man in front of me and spat in his face. He smiled angrily as he wiped my spit away.

"You're going to regret that," he said before backhanding me, making me hit my head hard against the wall behind me. I sucked in a sharp breath from the pain as it spread around my head like lightning.

"You better hope DeLuca answers my demands," he said with a smile.

"Or what?" I snapped. "Who the fuck are you?"

"Mario Castello, at your service, princess." He put his hand to his chest and tilted his head. *Prick.*

"What is your beef with Marcello?"

"He opened his mouth and stomped our family name in the mud," he answered through bared teeth. "He ruined my family, so I thought it only fair to ruin his."

"He won't waste his time on you. If he exposed you, it was for something you were doing to hurt his business or his family."

"He will if he wants his precious fiancée back."

I tried to think fast. I didn't know what this guy would do to me, but I knew I would get away somehow. I didn't want Marcello to walk into a trap. So I needed to think of something that would make him question his tactic and fast.

"You're going to be disappointed then. We can't stand each other. He won't pay a dime to you or your family." I snickered. "He would probably tell you to keep me."

"Well, according to Jacob and his fun pillow talk with that roommate of yours, you and Marc are in wove," he mocked.

"You're a fucking idiot, and so is Jacob. You won't get a dime."

Mario snarled and moved so that he was inches from my face. "You better pray he pays me my money, or you'll spend the rest of your days at the bottom of a six-foot hole in the middle of nowhere."

I reared back as much as I could to get away from his face. My adrenaline kicked in, making me laugh out loud. *Shit, why are you laughing? He's going to be pi—* My thought was interrupted with a right hook across my face, and all I saw was black.

Marcello ·

I watched the sun rise on our wedding day, and I still hadn't heard from Mila. My men were coming up short and taking a break to regroup. Dante had told me our father was getting pissed and had asked why I wasn't coming to the house. I didn't want to deal with the patriarchal bullshit on top of everything else. I was supposed to be getting ready for my wedding, but instead, I was in the same clothes as the day before, with no clue where my girl was.

I looked at the folder sitting on my desk. My wedding present to Mila. It held all of the necessary paperwork for her record label as well as paperwork for a loan from the bank and the perfect property for her studio. Everything was in her name, giving her full control. I wanted her to be happy and to lead a life she was proud of.

My phone rang, and my heart jumped. I answered after the first ring, not looking at the display.

"Mila?"

"Marcello, I'm so sorry," I heard a woman say on the other end.

"Who is this?"

"Harper."

I stood at the realization of who she was. She had to know where Mila was.

"Where is she?"

Harper started to cry. "I don't know. Something's wrong."

My heart dropped to the floor, and I thought I would vomit. Feeling myself falling to pieces, I plopped back into my chair and ran my hand through my hair.

"Tell me everything."

"We...we were leaving for New York," she started cautiously. Mila really was going to leave me. "My boyfriend was taking her to a diner outside the city while I went to her bachelorette party to buy us time. I was supposed to meet them when I pretended to go looking for her, but when I got to the diner, they weren't there. Now I can't get ahold of her or Jacob."

"She really was going to leave me," I said out loud, still processing what I had heard.

"She didn't want to, Marc," Harper explained. "She loves you so much. But her hate for the mafia and all that it entails was too much. She needed to get out before it was too late."

"Wait, did you say your boyfriend's name was Jacob?"

"Yeah, why?"

"What's his last name?" I asked with suspicion.

"Driver, why?"

"Shit." *Fucking Drivers.*

"What's going on, Marcello?"

My phone beeped to indicate another call.

"I need to take this call, Harper. Go to Anya and Aleksander's and wait there." I hung up and answered the incoming call. "What?"

"Now, now, that's no way to answer the phone," a familiar voice said.

"Who is this?"

"Your old pal, Mario Castillo. Listen, I have a beautiful new pet that I thought you would be interested in. We call her Mila."

"If you touch her, I'll cho—" I spit out, but Mario cut me off.

"You'll what, big man? If you don't do what I tell you, she will disappear, and you'll never find her." I growled into the phone in response. "You will bring me one-hundred million dollars within the next two hours, or your girl gets another love tap. If you call the cops, I will release her to my boys for some fun." I balled my hand into a fist so tight that my nails broke skin. The way he talked about Mila made my blood boil. "And,

Marcello, if you fail to bring me my money, your precious princess will never be found again. Don't fuck with me. I'll text you the coordinates."

The call ended and coordinates popped up right away. I wrote them down and stared at them for a moment, wondering how the hell we ended up here. I let out a deep roar as I threw my phone against the brick wall of my office and watched the glass shatter to the floor.

CHAPTER
SIXTEEN
MILA

I SQUINTED my eyes at the pain in my head. The sliver of light that came through the boarded-up window let me know it was daytime. Other than that, I had no idea what time it was or how long I had been missing. There was a bottle of water next to me, alongside an apple. I looked around to see if there was any way I could get out of the bedroom.

The door opened, and Jacob walked in.

"Oh goodie, it's you," I glared at him, then grimaced at the pain in my jaw from where Mario had punched me.

"Eek, you're looking worse for wear, princess."

"Maybe if you and Mario would stop hitting me, I could look a little more presentable."

"Sarcasm isn't as cute as you think it is," Jacob jabbed. *Idiot*.

"Why are you doing this? What about Harper?"

"Ahh, sweet Harper. I'll admit, she took me by surprise. I never thought I'd actually feel anything for her."

"So you just dated her to get to me?"

"Yeah, pretty much," he shrugged.

"Why are you helping this asshole? What do you have against Marcello and how do you even know him?" I wanted to understand and get as much information as I could.

"Marcello put my father behind bars. Mario and I met a few months back through some mutual friends, and when we got ta talkin', we realized we had a common enemy and thought it was time Marcello DeLuca paid for the shit he put our families through."

"You're both fucking delusional if you think you're coming out of this on top."

"It's adorable how much you trust him. Hopefully, you're the delusional one, for your sake," he snickered, then pointed to something next to me. "What, you're not hungry?"

I looked sideways at the water and apple. Just seeing the food made me want to throw up. *Why am I always so nauseous lately?* "My hands are tied behind my back, genius."

Jacob scowled at my remark, realizing I was right. He squatted down in front of me, and I hoped, for a brief moment, that he was untying me. Instead, he held the apple to my lips.

"C'mon, take a bite."

I glared at him for thinking he could feed me like an infant. I took a big bite, chewed it up, and spit the food into his smirking face.

"You bitch!"

He threw the apple across the room and kicked the bottle of water after it. The commotion brought the attention of Mario, who walked into the room.

"Having trouble with our guest?"

"She spit food at me," Jacob complained.

"Don't be a whiney bitch," I cut out.

Jacob took a step toward me, his fists balled, but Mario stopped him. "I think she's had enough for now, don't you?"

Jacob sucked his teeth at me before storming out of the room. Then Mario walked over to grab the bottle of water and walked it back to me.

"If I untie you, will you behave?"

I just stared at him, not uttering a word. I didn't know who was in the other room, so I wouldn't make a move. Not yet. Mario must have come to the same conclusion, because he leaned in to cut the binds around my wrists, then my ankles. I rubbed my raw skin where the rope had cut into me. Mario opened the water and held it in front of me. I didn't realize how thirsty I was until I took a drink. I emptied the bottle quickly but then realized it was a mistake to drink it so fast.

"I'm going to be sick," I warned as I stopped bile from coming up.

"Jesus, that's gross."

"Is there a bathroom?" I urged.

"Come on."

Mario helped me up but didn't take his hand off my arm. When he led me out of the bedroom, I realized we were in some sort of old hunting cabin. It reminded me of Lake Tahoe. Five other guys sat around the cabin, playing cards or scrolling on their phones. Jacob watched from a chair in the corner as Mario walked me to the small bathroom.

"Don't get any ideas. There are more of my guys outside," Mario warned before shutting the door behind me.

I quickly locked the door and turned to the toilet to empty my stomach. When I was done, I moved to the sink to wash out my mouth. Taking advantage of time alone in the bathroom, I looked at my reflection in the dirty mirror. Seeing the bruises made me glad it wasn't a clear view. I lightly touched the tender skin, wincing at the slightest pressure. Then I rummaged through the cabinet and small drawers in hopes of finding something to help, but it was all empty.

I jumped at the sound of someone banging on the door. "Time's up, princess," Mario yelled through the door.

"Just a minute," I yelled back.

I looked around and saw there was nothing I could use to my advantage, and the window was too small to fit through. So I hurried and used the toilet before unlocking the door. The second he heard the lock open, he opened the door and looked around.

"Let's go," he said as he grabbed my arm and shoved me back into the bedroom.

He closed the door, and I heard a chair sliding across the floor before thumping against the door. *Barricaded, great.*

I looked around the room again, still hopeful that I might find a way out. I crept across the room to the window to see how well it was boarded. I wiggled a wood plank, trying to stay calm at the realization that I could jimmy it free. I just needed an opportunity to get the planks off without drawing attention.

As if on cue, music blared through the cabin from the main area. I heard cheers and what sounded like the popping of cans. I couldn't tell if more men had joined or if it was the same that were there earlier. But it didn't matter. Their music was loud enough that they would never hear if I pulled the wood free from the window frame. I didn't care that there could be guys outside. I only knew that I needed to try to get free.

Marcello

I tore off to my father's house to grab my brothers and all the men I could scrounge up. Mila was in the hands of someone who was not very intelligent but dumb enough to truly endanger her life. Cristiano stopped me as I stormed into the house.

"Where the hell have you been?"

"Busy," I answered and tried to move past him, but he stopped me. Dante and Dominic walked in from behind him.

"Father is irate. You should have been here, coming up with a plan, instead of sulking around your house like a brokenhearted little boy."

"Easy, Cris," Dante stepped in before I could respond. "Can't you see he's on a mission?"

"Tell us what you need, Marc." Dominic stepped in closer.

"I know where Mila is."

"Where?" Dante asked.

"Fucking Mario Castillo and Jacob Driver took her for ransom," I answered, looking square into Cristiano's face. I hated how he acted like our father, especially at that moment. I wanted to lay him out.

"So, she didn't tuck tail and run away," Cristiano joked. I didn't correct him. The details of how Mila had come to be missing was between her and I.

"Back off, Cris," Dante snapped in annoyance. "What did they say? Why did they take her?"

"Mario's still pissed I exposed them for laundering money, and I'm sure Jacob wants revenge for his dad going to prison."

"When will these guys learn not to go against us?"

Dominic asked, wanting to be a part of the conversation.

"How much did they ask for?" Cristiano asked, crossing his arms in front of him.

"Hundred million."

Dante whistled, and Dominic laughed while Cristiano just raised his eyebrows.

"We would never pay that," Cris admitted.

"She's his fiancée and the Don's daughter," Dominic interjected.

"Then the Don can pay her ransom," Cristiano yelled. "They aren't married yet, and she's not family. Mario won't be getting his money."

"Watch yourself, Cris," I warned, stepping into his face. "We may not be married yet, but we will be. You will not disregard this and keep her life hanging in the balance over some petty bullshit you have stewing in that big head of yours." My brother and I stared at one another for a moment. When I knew he had understood me, I stepped back and continued to explain the rest to my brothers. "He sent me the coordinates of where to meet for the exchange. He's a fucking idiot, so I'm assuming he didn't think to use a location separate from where he's holding her. I came here for you guys, and whoever else will come, to go get Mila back."

"I'm on it," Dominic said before taking out his phone and sending a text to our men.

"I'll stay here with father in case anything else happens," Cristiano said curtly, then turned and walked back into the house.

"Don't let him get to you," Dante tried to settle me. "He's never going to stop kissing dad's ass."

"Okay! We have twelve guys on their way. Is that enough?" Dominic asked.

"That'll work. Let's go get your girl, Marc."

Within an hour, my team and I were sneaking through the woods on the edge of the city. Five more guys showed up to meet us and agreed to hang out in the woods in case Mario's men tried to scatter. We quietly surrounded the tattered cabin where music echoed through the trees. Dante, Dominic, and three other men followed me to the front door. I didn't bother to knock. I just kicked the door in.

My eyes fell on Mario first, and I headed straight to him as my brothers tussled with the other men. Dante threw Jacob through a window just as I grabbed Mario by his shirt and punched him in the face but didn't let him go.

"Where's Mila?"

Mario spit blood onto the floor. "Where's my money, asshole?"

I punched him a couple more times, then held him straight to ask him once more, "Where the fuck is Mila?"

He had trouble keeping his head up as he pointed to a door with a chair wedged under the handle. I shoved Mario off to Dominic, who had walked up to us.

"Tie his hands," I ordered as I threw the chair out of the way and busted into the bedroom. My heart raced at the opportunity to hold my girl. "Mila?" I looked around the room and realized she wasn't there. I hit the door with the end of my fist as I stalked back out to Mario, who was being led out of the cabin. "Where the fuck is she?" I yelled as I yanked him from my brother to make him face me.

"Sh—she should be there. We didn't move her," Mario answered, scared. "She must have escaped somehow."

I roared in anger as I shoved Mario back to my

brother, worried about what I would do if I kept him too close to me. I looked around at the chaos around the cabin, happy to see we had the majority of Mario's guys down and tied up. Dante walked up with a bloody Jacob.

"Where's Mila?"

"She got away somehow. They have no idea where she is," I answered as I looked around, trying to figure out where she would run.

"Here, take him to the truck," Dante ordered as he handed Jacob off to one of our men. "Dom, you take Mario to the truck with some of the others. Marc and I will get a few of the guys and go look for her."

I nodded at Dante, and we grabbed three other men to figure out where to start. It sounded as though they were a million miles away as my mind drifted to Mila. I worried she would be hurt and alone out in the woods. I worried she thought I had given up on her and that I would never see her again. That couldn't happen. There was no way she was gone for good.

"Marcello," Dante snapped his fingers in my face, bringing me back to the moment. "You good?"

"Yeah, what'd you come up with?"

"Since she got out of the only window of the bedroom, and it's at the opposite end of the entrance, we think she would have run in that direction, back toward the road," Dante explained as he pointed to the left of us.

"Alright, let's go."

We spread out and searched the area between the cabin and the road. I heard a scuffle here and there from my men finding Mario's stragglers, but I never saw anything that hinted that Mila might have gone in the direction I was searching. The sun was setting as I stepped out onto the road and headed toward the trucks. The other guys had come out of the woods when I approached the vehicles, all empty handed. *Shit.* I waited a few minutes and began to worry more. I didn't know how many men Mario had with him, and I didn't see Dante coming out of the woods.

"Where's my brother?"

CHAPTER
SEVENTEEN

MILA

I RAN AS FAST as I could the moment my feet hit the ground. My heart was racing as I fled the cabin, swiveling my head to make sure I wasn't being followed. I realized I was in the middle of the woods and started to panic. Where could I hide? I had no idea where I was. I turned to look behind me to make sure no one was following me, when I was suddenly on the ground.

I groaned in pain as I looked at my feet to see I had tripped over a large root coming out of the ground from a tree next to me. I thought I heard someone coming and looked around in a frenzy. My eyes fell on an old, decaying shed that didn't look large enough to even hold a riding lawn mower. It was, however, big enough to hide me.

I scrambled to my feet and ran to the shed, thankful that it was mostly covered from trees and overgrowth of the vegetation. My heart jumped into my throat when I heard voices just as I closed the tiny door of the shed. I peeked through a hole and slapped my hand over my mouth when I saw Marcello and his brothers walking toward the cabin. They had a dozen or more men with them. I almost yelled out for them but decided against it. Yes, it would be hell to find my way out of the woods, but it would be worse for me to be taken back to my father. He would be determined to make my life hell. I sat in the corner of the shed, praying I wouldn't find any creatures keeping me company.

Not long after Marcello and his men walked by, I heard a loud commotion through the woods as men were running towards the direction Marcello had come from and others were fighting. I watched from my hiding spot, debating with myself about coming out. I knew I would be safe with Marcello, but I couldn't face him. I had chosen to leave instead of staying with him and still hadn't changed my mind, especially after being taken by Mario. My heart hurt for Harper as I thought about Jacob betraying her like that. She seemed so happy.

I watched Marcello's men ushering Mario's guys back to the direction they had come from, figuring that must be the way to a road. Then, Dominic walked by with Mario beaten and tied. I silently wished I had the chance to add to his bruises. Shortly after, Marcello and some of his guys walked back, obviously searching for me. I could see the worry on Marc's face, and my stomach twisted. I wanted to run to him so badly.

When I thought I had waited long enough for Marcello to load up and leave, I crept out of my hiding spot. The sun was setting, and visibility wasn't great. I had only taken a few steps when I was tackled to the ground.

"There she is," the guy breathed as I fought against him, but he was too strong. He held my wrists and turned me to my back, straddling me to keep me still and holding my arms to the ground. "You've created a mess."

"Get off of me!" I hollered as I maneuvered my legs, trying to get free.

"I don't think so, sweetheart. You're gonna pay for my trouble." The guy started leaning in as if he was going to kiss me before he was yanked backward and off me. I sat up and scooted back as I watched Dante knock the guy out and drop him to the ground.

"We've been looking everywhere for you."

"Please, don't tell Marcello you found me," I begged as I got to my feet.

"Why the hell not? He's torn up about you going missing."

"I can't go back. At least not yet. I just need some time to think. Please."

Dante studied me for a moment. He then took a deep breath and brought out his phone, dialed a number, and held it up to his ear, not taking his eyes off me.

"Dom, tell Marc I'm okay and to head back to the warehouse. I'm going to look around the cabin a bit more to see if I can find traces of Mila." He was silent for a moment as his brother talked on the other end. "No, tell him to go back with you. I'll call if I find anything."

Dante ended the call and did something on his phone before putting it back in his pocket.

"Thank you," I gushed.

"I'll take you somewhere to shower and rest. Come on."

"It's fine," I urged, worried he would tell his brother where he was taking me. "I can find a ride."

"Not a chance, Mila. I'll promise you that I won't say a word to my brother, as long as you agree to stick with me. It's too dangerous for you to be alone right now. You need to be protected."

"Dante, but—" I began to protest.

"I'm not afraid to throw you over my shoulder and walk you right into Marcello's arms," he warned. *Shit.*

"Fine, but not a word to anyone. Dominic would tell Marcello without hesitation."

"I don't break my promises."

I held out my arm, telling him to lead the way, and followed him through the woods and out onto the road. We walked a little way before a car came to stop beside us, spiking my anxiety. On instinct, I grabbed Dante's arm like a vice.

"Easy, Mila. It's just our Uber."

I released his arm and let him help me into the backseat. Getting inside, he asked the driver to take us to a hotel in the middle of the city, but not a high-end one. It was sketchy enough to not have cameras and accepted cash and a false name at check-in.

"At least it's a step up from the cabin," I joked as we walked into the room and looked around.

Dante looked in the bathroom and called me over. "It's actually pretty clean in here. Why don't you take a bath and relax while I order us some food?"

"Are you sure no one will find us here?"

"I promise. And I'll be right here, just in case."

He nodded his head at me to ensure he meant it before closing the door behind him. I turned on the water to fill the tub and undress. My limbs suddenly felt like jelly at the prospect of being able to relax. I lowered myself into the hot water and just focused on my breathing for a moment, which became labored as I fought the tears that wanted to come, and my throat started to sting. Not able to hold it in, I let out a cry that led to bawling my eyes out. I was so stressed out and terrified and relieved all at the same time. It was too much. I was grateful to be alive and safe but broken for hurting Marcello so badly. I was scared about going back to my father's house and what he would do while desperate to be in Marcello's arms. It was all just too much.

I leaned back against the back of the tub and slid down until the water was up to my chin. I cried until it hurt, and I had nothing left. I closed my eyes for a moment but must have fallen asleep because when I opened them again, the water was lukewarm. A knock on the door made me jump.

"You okay?" Dante asked through the door.

"Yes," I answered back.

"Food's here if you want to eat it while it's hot."

"Okay!"

I used the cheap shampoo and bar soap provided by the hotel to wash myself, then dressed back in the gross clothes I had on before. With the towel twisted in my hair, I opened the door but was met with a bag in my face.

"I got you new clothes," Dante said without looking at me.

I thanked him, took the bag, and closed the door again. I smiled when I saw that he had gotten me new underwear, socks, and a couple pairs of leggings, t-shirts, and hoodies. I didn't want to know how he got my size right — I was just grateful he thought of it.

When I emerged, I couldn't believe what I was seeing. Dante had somehow transformed the room into something decent. He had new bedding on the king-sized bed, a new larger television, along with a new table and chairs. He even threw in a recliner, which I guessed was for him, and a new lamp.

"How did you get all of this here?"

"I paid the Uber driver extra to do some shopping," Dante answered from the table where he was opening multiple containers of Chinese food. "Come eat. I got you some water and power drinks there in the fridge."

I looked where he pointed and saw a small fridge tucked in the corner. I was impressed with his thoughtfulness. I sat down with him to eat, hearing my stomach grumble from being so empty.

"Listen, I know I told you to stick with me, but I have to get back to Marcello before he starts to worry," Dante explained between bites of orange chicken and rice. "I paid for a week for you to stay here and will have a guy parked at the end of the lot at all times. He won't tell anyone where he is or why."

"You told him I was here?" I shrieked in panic.

"No, Mila. Relax. I just told him I was keeping someone for the Don until we needed him." I snickered at Dante using my father in a lie. Classic fear tactic. "I'll go back home and keep them distracted for a short time while you figure your shit out."

"Thanks for doing all of this, Dante. I know it's a lot."

"You're part of the family," he shrugged before taking another bite.

We ate in silence for a bit. I was mulling over all the events that had happened in the last couple weeks and how much things had changed and spiraled out of control. I thought about how Marcello had opened up to me and softened before my eyes, turning into a new man. I thought about how much I loved him and how much my body and heart ached for him.

"You know, Marcello may come across as an angry bear, but he's not always like that. After our mother died, he poured everything into work and to become a warrior for our father. He was crushed when she died and was determined to never let anyone close enough to make him feel that hurt again. Until you." I stared at Dante with tears pooling in my eyes. "He loves you somethin' fierce, Mila. Enough to risk our fall to let you go and find happiness. Enough to break his heart on purpose by letting you go. But I pray you change your mind and give him a chance."

Dante stood and took care of his plate, then walked to the door. "Stay in your room and don't call anyone. I will stop by in a couple of days to check on you. Keep this on the handle and don't let housekeeping inside," he said as he put a 'do not disturb' sign on the door handle. "I'll have food brought to you twice a day. If you need anything, run to the red Chevy at the opposite end of the parking lot, and he will call me."

"Wait, have you heard anything about Harper?"

"She's fine. She's with Anya. You should know that she told Marcello about your plan to move to New York." *That stung.*

"It's complicated," was all I could say.

"I know it is. I just wanted you to know that he knew."

"Thanks again, for all of this, Dante."

"See ya soon, Mila.

Two days had passed, and I was climbing the walls. Dante had some pain reliever and a couple of books delivered with breakfast the day before, but I couldn't focus enough to read. Luckily, he had activated some of his streaming accounts on the smart TV he had bought, and I was able to watch movies. Needing to feel a connection to the outside world, I changed to a local TV station that was covering the news, and I couldn't believe what I was seeing. George Martin's face was on the screen in a mugshot, followed by a video of him being arrested. The reporter stated he was being charged with five counts of sexual assault but was suspected of being guilty of more.

"Holy shit. Marcello was right," I said out loud.

I was suddenly hit with a round of nausea and had to run to the bathroom. I groaned loudly as I sat next to the toilet and leaned my head against the wall. I couldn't understand why I was feeling so sick, until something clicked into place. The thought brought more of my lunch up. I counted the days in my head and stared at the sink in disbelief.

"I think I'm *pregnant.*"

CHAPTER
EIGHTEEN

MILA

I LAID in bed all day, going over every scenario possible for my future. Admittedly, some were nice and involved Marcello and I living happily ever after with three children, a dog, and a white picket fence. Of course, I thought that would be the one farthest from reality since it was what I wanted most.

I was six episodes deep in some vampire show when there was a knock at the door. I sat up straight and listened to see if they knocked again, and they did. I got up and peeked through the hole in the door, relieved to see Dante on the other side.

"About time," I chided as he walked in. "I was going stir crazy. I need to get out of here."

"Mila, I need you to listen to me."

"What happened?" I looked Dante over for any signs of stress, but all I saw was annoyance.

"Marcello is freaking the fuck out, and I hate seeing him so distraught. We need to tell him you're here and alright."

I paced the floor in thought. I knew I needed to see Marcello, especially with the chance that I was pregnant. "Alright. You can tell him where I am. But I need you to do me a favor first."

"What's that?"

"I need Harper."

"I'm crushed, bella. I was certain that I would be the first person you would ask for," Marcello's voice sounded from the door.

I turned in shock at seeing my six-foot prince staring at me with a haunted look on his face. His hair was a mess, and his face was full of dark stubble. Realizing Marc was truly in front of me, I turned to Dante.

"You said you don't break promises!"

"I don't," he urged.

"I followed him," Marcello answered. He stepped fully into the hotel room and let the door slam shut. "I knew he was up to something, but I never would have thought it was this."

"Easy, brother. There is a lot you and Mila need to talk about. Once you hear what she has to say, you can come at me," Dante said as he held his hands up in surrender and quickly left me alone with Marcello.

"Traitor!" I yelled after him. I wanted to see Marcello, but I thought I would have time to prepare myself. I definitely didn't think the version of him I saw would be what greeted me. It pulled at my heart that I was the one to make him look so miserable.

"How could you leave me, Mila?" he asked as he walked over to stand in front of me.

He was angry, but his face fell as he really looked at me. I knew he was looking at the bruises on my face and my jaw, which was slightly swollen. He raised his hand as if he was going to touch me but decided against it and let his hand fall to his side.

"It was selfish to leave in the middle of the night, knowing what kind of chaos and recoil it would bring," he continued with his rant. He turned away from me and began pacing as he talked. "Our fathers are at each other's throats, Mila."

"Of course, all you care about is the fucking family business," I scoffed.

"I care about you!" he yelled as he walked back to stand in front of me. "It tore me up thinking about what could have happened to you. I was ready to let everything crumble and walk away if it meant you were safe."

I stared into Marcello's beautiful, honey eyes that were red-rimmed and tired. My heart stuck in my throat at the realization of how much he loved me. How much pain I had caused by being stubborn instead of talking to him about everything first.

"You didn't even give me a chance to try to make you happy."

"I'm sorry," I choked out as tears fell. I was shocked to see his fall as well. "You're right, I was selfish. After Costa Rica, I thought there would be no way out if I married you, and I couldn't give up on myself like that."

"But you could give up on me?"

"It wasn't like that," I cried out. "I love you so much, Marc. It tore me up to walk away from you. But I knew that if I left my destiny in my father's hands, I would be miserable."

"I'm the one your destiny would be tied with, and I'm not your father."

Marcello pulled a folder from behind him and shoved it toward me. "What's this?" I asked.

"Open it."

I sat on the corner of the bed and opened the worn, blue folder. As I looked over the documents, new tears fell. He had arranged everything for me to have my own record label and studio.

"This was your wedding gift," he said as he sat down next to me. "Mila, I want to give you the world. I would never keep you from your dreams. I was already finding ways to change the way we do business and to take charge of everything so that you wouldn't have to be a part of any of it."

"I will always be a part of this world as your wife. There will always be people you pissed off that will want to use me as leverage."

"It will never happen again, Mila. I promise you that I will do everything in my power to keep you out of it and safe. You have my word. I love you so much it hurts."

I sat in silence, letting his words sink it. "Is that why George was arrested?" I asked.

"That's just the start, bella. Mario and Jacob will follow along, with all of his friends that helped take you. Your safety is my priority." He lightly ran the back of his finger against my cheek, the one that wasn't bruised. "I love you so much, Mila. You have made me feel whole and safe, which I never thought I would experience. You are my home, Mila. But I understand if you want to go or if you still don't feel safe. I won't keep you here and have you resent me for the rest of your life. If you want to leave, I won't stop you. I'll make sure your father leaves you alone and that you aren't bothered."

I started crying all over again at his admission. *How could I leave this man?* Without a word, I climbed onto his lap and kissed him fiercely. His arms wrapped around me tightly, like he was afraid I would drift away. When we parted for air, I rested my forehead to his and scratched his stubble.

"I love you, Marc. I'm not going anywhere."

He kissed me again as he turned me to lie on the bed. "Say it again," he said against my skin as he kissed my neck.

"I'm staying," I laughed out when he blew strawberries into my neck.

He feathered kisses back up to my lips and readjusted us, so we were fully on the bed. He caressed my breasts as he ground his erection into my thigh. I sat up to lift my t-shirt over my head, and when Marc discovered I was braless, he took one of my nipples into his mouth and sucked. I laid back as he worshipped my mounds and slid a large hand into my leggings. He moaned into my skin when he felt how wet I was.

"Always ready," he grinned as he moved his way down my legs, taking my leggings and panties with him.

He spread my thighs and settled between them, kissing each leg before blowing air onto my sensitive nub. When I wiggled my hips at the sensation, he smiled at me before diving in. I let my head fall back as he devoured my overly sensitive pussy, adding two fingers to fill me up. I reached down and threaded my fingers into his hair, making sure he didn't pull away until I was soaking his face. Within seconds, I was calling out his name and shaking from an intense orgasm.

He quickly stood and undressed, but before he could get on the bed, I sat up and took his gorgeous cock into my mouth, grabbing his ass cheeks so that he couldn't move. I heard him let out a moan as he lightly grabbed a handful of hair at the back of my head.

"Only for a minute, bella. I need to be inside you," he groaned.

I sucked and licked, wondering how long he would

let me play before he took over, but I didn't have to wonder long. He lightly pushed my shoulders back, letting me know he couldn't wait any longer. I smiled up at him as I scooted back and laid down. He climbed over me and shoved his cock into my eager kitty. He kissed me passionately as he hammered into me, neither of us able to get close enough to one another. Reaching down to pull my knees to my chest for a better angle, he then thrusted as deep as he could go and held it, rocking a little until I begged him for more.

"Fuck me, Marc," I moaned with need.

He smiled down at me as he moved my legs over his shoulders and started slamming into me from a push-up position. The room filled with the sound of our skin smacking together and our labored breathing. I was so close, so I reached between us to rub my clit for more friction, bringing me to another climax.

"Fuck, bella," Marc growled as my walls tightened round him.

He pumped into me a few more times before emptying his load into me. Then he laid on top of me for a moment as I traced circles on his back and regained my breathing. The possibility of me being pregnant invaded my mind, and my throat closed. *Well, now's as good a time as any.*

"I think I'm pregnant," I let out and held my breath for his response.

I felt him chuckle, but he didn't move. "It doesn't work that fast, my love."

"I'm being serious, Marcello."

This time, he raised himself up on his arms to look at me with his brow furrowed. "What are you saying to me?"

"I need to get tested, but I am pretty sure I'm pregnant," I answered, showing my teeth in a worried grin.

Marcello let out a high-pitched laugh and jumped to his feet. He looked the happiest I had ever seen him as he walked around in a circle, his hands buried in his hair.

"Wait," he started and came to a stop in front of me. "Did you know this before you left?"

"No. I didn't realize it until I was here."

Marc rushed up and kissed me fast and hard. "We're gonna have a baby!"

His excitement was contagious. I sat up in the bed and laughed with him. I was so scared he would be upset about the news, but he surprised me again. I should never have questioned his love for me or that he wanted to start a life with me. I should have trusted he would do all he could to make me happy.

Once we were settled, we showered together, enjoying each other's bodies once more. I was impressed with Marcello's ability to rally and come again as well as his stamina and strength to keep us from slipping on wet porcelain. When we were done, we dressed and started gathering my things to leave.

"I need to see Harper," I told Marc as I folded my clothes and handed them to him to place in the bag he was holding.

"She's at your apartment. Do you want me to take you there?"

"Is she okay?"

"Dante's been checking in on her. She's pissed about Jacob but doesn't blame anyone. He fooled everyone."

"I need to see her, but I want to stay with you tonight. Can you just drop me off for a couple of hours?"

"Whatever you need, princess," he promised with a kiss on the tip of my nose.

We decided to leave everything in the hotel room except for the clothes. It needed an upgrade anyway. Marc dropped me off at my apartment, but I could tell he was having a hard time leaving. Truth be told, it was hard for me too. Reluctantly, I left Marcello to run his errands while I checked in with my bestie.

The second I opened the door, she pulled me into her arms.

"Holy shit! I thought you were dead!"

"I'm alive and well," I answered with a light laugh.

She stepped back and held me at arm's length but sucked in a sharp breath when she saw my face. "Jesus, Mila. Does it hurt?"

"Obviously," I snorted as I moved to sit on the couch. I had lounged in the hotel room for two days, but my exercise with Marc left me feeling a little weak.

"Tell me everything," Harper demanded as she sat next to me on the couch.

I told her everything about Mario and Jacob and how I escaped. She shared how Dante explained why Jacob would pull such a stunt, then kept creeping around our apartment to make sure she was alright. I told her about Dante saving me and hiding me away until Marcello drove him crazy. I also told her that I was staying and couldn't leave Marcello.

"Are you sure you're okay with not moving to New York?"

"I'm fine, girl. I just wanted to be with you and make sure you wouldn't be alone."

"I love you. Harper."

"Aw, I love you too."

I packed a few days' worth of clothes and toiletries after I called Marcello from Harper's phone and told him to pick me up. We planned to go buy me a new one the next day. I hugged my best friend goodbye and headed to Marc's suite. It was nostalgic to be back in the place where I lost my virginity to the man of my dreams.

"I want to show you something," Marcello whispered as he ushered me toward the master bathroom. When he turned on the light, I saw three different pregnancy tests sitting on the counter. "I picked them up while I was waiting for you to call me. I also grabbed some ice cream and pickles."

"That's an old wives' tale, silly."

"I wanted to be prepared," he shrugged. "So?"

"Do you want to watch me pee on these?" I teased.

"It wouldn't bother me," he answered honestly.

"We're not there yet, tiger." I playfully pushed him out of the bathroom. "I'll be right out."

"Don't look at them without me," he rushed as I closed the door on him, giggling at how adorable he was acting.

When I was done, I opened the door again to find him standing there with his hands resting on the doorframe.

"Impatient much?"

"What do they say?" He rushed past me and looked at the sticks sitting on the counter.

"Another minute, and we will know." I smiled and stepped up to the counter next to him, letting him fold me into his side.

We both watched the displays change, and my throat went dry. All three said the same thing. We were pregnant. Marcello picked me up and spun me around. When he placed me back firmly on my feet, he dropped to his knees, lifted my shirt, and kissed my belly.

"I can't wait to meet you, little guy," he whispered.

"Or girl," I chided, making him smile up at me. He stood and kissed me deeply.

"I can't wait to start our life, bella." He kissed my forehead. "To see you in that white dress and announce to the world that you're mine." He kissed the tip of my nose. "To watch your belly grow with our child inside." He kissed my cheek. "And then to try as often as possible to give them siblings." We both laughed as he kissed my other cheek. "I feel like I can finally live, Mila."

"I can't wait to see how our life unfolds. I love you, Marc."

EPILOGUE

MARCELLO

"MILA, COME ON! WE'RE LATE!" Anya scolded from behind me.

"I'm just putting on my earrings," I answered.

I took a step back and took one more look in the large mirror. My wedding dress still fit and looked more beautiful than I had remembered.

"You look angelic," Anya doted.

"She looks hot!" Harper chimed in with her bouquet and mine in her hands. "Now let's go."

The three of us hurried through the halls until we were in line. I saw Dante look Harper up and down as she took her place beside him, making me chuckle.

I stood nervously, spinning my flowers in my hands. I felt a hand on my back, making me jump and turn to see who was sneaking up on me.

"Easy, my daughter. It's just me." My father looked me up and down with a look of admiration. "You look beautiful, Mila. Stunning."

"Thank you, papa."

"I never told you how proud I am of you. And that you are safe and happy." Tears threatened to fall, but I managed to hold them back to salvage my makeup. "And perhaps I don't say this enough, but I love you."

"I love you, too, papa."

The music started, and the line ahead of us moved. I was overjoyed to hear such affection from my father. When it was our turn, my father rested my hand on his arm.

"Are you ready?"

"More than ever."

My father walked me down the aisle of a beautiful church, the pews were filled with witnesses to our wedding. I knew the church was full, but all I could see was Marcello, smiling like a lunatic at the end of the aisle with our family and friends standing beside him. He was so handsome in his tailored tux and his hair styled to perfection. I couldn't believe that he was mine, and I was his, and that we were about to solidify our union for life.

"You're breathtaking," Marc whispered to me as I walked up to him.

"You look pretty handsome yourself."

I could barely get through the ceremony but managed not to mess it up. We humored the photographer for more photos before heading to the reception. The hall Anya picked out was amazing, and she had decorated it beautifully.

We laughed and cried through everyone's speeches and picked at the amazing food. Harper was on the dance floor with a kid that wasn't a day over three, twirling him around in circles, making him squeal.

"Look at Dante," Marcello whispered in my ear.

When I looked down the table, Dante was staring at Harper with the goofiest expression on his face.

"It's time, ladies and gentlemen," a voice boomed

over the speakers. "For the bride and groom's first dance."

Everyone cheered, then clinked their glasses to get us to kiss. When we were in the middle of the floor, Marc bent me over for a theatrical kiss. He held our pose as our guests cheered and the photographer could take a few photos. When we stood upright, the music started, and my heart swelled. John Legend serenaded us as we swayed together to the music.

"You have all of me, bella," Marc whispered softly, his face full of emotion.

"And you me."

"I love you, Mrs. DeLuca." Marc's smile grew across his face to match mine.

"I love you, Mr. Fedorov," I teased. He laughed out loud as he spun me around, making me shriek with laughter, and everyone joined in to dance and celebrate this magical day with us.

Thank you so much for reading! If you enjoyed Mila and Marcello's story, you can get the Bonus Scene here: https://bf.rubyemhart.com/a102jtk659

DID YOU LIKE THIS BOOK?
THEN YOU'LL LOVE

ACCIDENTAL VEGAS DADDY
An Enemies to Lovers Best Friend's Brother Romance

I accidentally married my best friend's brother in Vegas.
Now I'm pregnant.
"Three million dollars. Going once, twice. SOLD!"
"To the tall gentleman in the back."

A bachelorette auction, a blurry night in the city of Sin.
Wickedly hot stranger in my bed and,
A *huge* rock on my finger. WTF! I'm *married*?
Shocked, I fled the city with my dirty little secret.

A week later...

My BFF invited me to her welcome home party.
In walks Mason Russell, a certified playboy billionaire.
Turns out, he's not only my Vegas husband, but my
best friend's brother.

The plan was to end the facade but,
His seductive green eyes and bulging biceps have me
melting into his arms.

He's a bachelor that can't be tamed, but
What will happen when I tell him he's going to be a
daddy?

**Click below to start reading
Accidental Vegas Daddy!**
https://www.amazon.com/dp/B0BT6ZKJ6V

THANK YOU FOR READING

ONE BOSSY ARRANGEMENT!

If you enjoyed Mila and Marcello's story, you can get the Bonus Scene here:
https://bf.rubyemhart.com/a102jtk659

Find me at:
Website: rubyemhart.com
Amazon Author Page: https://www.amazon.com/Ruby-Emhart/e/B0B8411ZSR
VIP Newsletter: rubyemhart.com
TikTok: https://www.tiktok.com/@rubyemhartauthor
Facebook: facebook.com/rubyemhart
Instagram: instagram.com/rubyemhartauthor
Booksprout: https://booksprout.co/reviewer/author/view/31224/ruby-emhart
Goodreads: https://www.goodreads.com/author/show/22666504.Ruby_Emhart
Bookbub: https://www.bookbub.com/authors/ruby-emhart
Get My FREE Book: https://dl.bookfunnel.com/9319a8co04

My Books:
Accidental Vegas Daddy: An Enemies to Lovers Best Friend's Brother Romance https://www.amazon.com/dp/B0BT6ZKJ6V
Claimed By My Billionaire Ex: A Brother's Best Friend Secret Baby Romance
https://www.amazon.com/dp/B0BR835HVZ
Bossy Grump Billionaires: A complete Enemies to Lovers Accidental Pregnancy Romance Collection: https://www.amazon.com/dp/B0BPMHC8BS
Mistletoe Grump: An Enemies to Lovers Holiday Romance:
https://www.amazon.com/dp/B0BN27PCW3
Grump Daddy Next Door: An Enemies to Lovers Pretend Relationship:
https://www.amazon.com/gp/product/B0BLHVPK6Z
Doctor Bossy Grump: An Enemies to Lovers Age Gap Romance:
https://www.amazon.com/gp/product/B0BH92C9XZ
Secret Babies for a Bossy Grump: An Enemies to Lovers Romance:
https://www.amazon.com/gp/product/B0BD78DXCR
Ex-Boyfriend Bosshole: An Enemies to Lovers Romance:
https://www.amazon.com/gp/product/B0B853PCZH

If you want more fun Boston billionaire's steamy romance, check out my upcoming new release *Secret Daddy Grump*.

Turn the page for an excerpt from *Secret Daddy Grump*.

EXCERPT FROM SECRET DADDY GRUMP

I THREW one arm around his shoulder and extended the other to feel our way out of the elevator and to my apartment. His lips were plush and soft, but his demeanor was anything but. He kissed me like I was his last meal on earth, grabbing me by the waist and leaving the navigating up to me. We miraculously made it to my door, and he pressed me up against it, his hands wandering down to settle at my ass. Dazed, I fished my keys out of my purse. I tore myself away from him and gave myself a moment to look at him. His pupils were dilated to no end and his cheeks were slightly flushed. God, he's beautiful. He cupped my cheek with one hand, leaning back in to murmur against my lips, "open the fucking door."

I had gotten completely lost in his beauty. I fumbled with the keys to unlock the door and the stranger – which, now that I think about it, this whole thing is definitely unprofessional – wasted no time in pulling the both of us in and slamming the door closed. My apartment was dark, so I took him by the wrist and let my muscle memory guide us to my bedroom.

We reached my bed, and I turned on a small bedside

lamp. He pushed me onto the blankets and stood at my legs, taking his leather jacket off and tossing it over my desk chair nearby. Under this dim lighting, he was nothing short of gorgeous. His eyes borderline glowed as they burned through me, and it was then that I realized exactly what I was doing. It's whatever, I deserve a treat, don't I?

"Are you going to stare at me for long?" My voice trailed off, and my heart quickened in my chest. I couldn't deal with his hungry gaze for much longer. I needed more.

ABOUT THE AUTHOR

I have always been a sucker for sappy love stories with perfect dream-like endings.
The truth is – love is complicated, painful at times but it takes you to places you have never been before.
I found my ultimate tickle and flutter at the heart with steamy contemporary romance.
As an avid reader I just live and breathe books, especially everything romantic.
I dig into scenes for all the big too-hot-to-handle feels so you can discover steamy romance with sizzling-hot actions and the perfect combos of heart, flirt, humor filled with a high dose of happily-ever-afters.
I am a coastal gal residing with my husband, our two sons and our fox-like-pup.
I really fancy dancing and listening to all tunes from the 1980's including people watching, coffee and pastry from different patisserie (to satisfy my very sweet tooth). I love fruits, wine tasting, walking/hiking and traveling with my most excellent family.
Just saying!

amazon.com/Ruby-Emhart/e/B0B8411ZSR

tiktok.com/@rubyemhartauthor

facebook.com/rubyemhart

instagram.com/rubyemhartauthor

bookbub.com/authors/ruby-emhart

Printed in Great Britain
by Amazon

21295939R00112